1

For my mother

Iona Boy

MARY RHIND

The New Iona Press

Acknowledgements
The author would like to thank Jean Watt for help with editing, Ian Rhind for help with the map and Dr Colm O Baoill for advice on pronunciation of names.

British Library Cataloguing in Publication Data.
A catalogue record for this book is available from the British Library.
ISBN 0 9516283 7 2

Typeset by XL Publishing Services, Nairn
Printed in Great Britain by
Highland Printers, Inverness
for
The New Iona Press
7 Drynie Terrace, Inverness IV2 4UP

Contents

	Map	vi
1.	Kidnap!	1
2.	A Strange Shore	14
3.	The Crane Cleric	29
4.	Omens of Doom	43
5.	A Royal Feast	56
6.	Lìos Mòr	71
7.	The Forest of Gloom	86
8.	Wild Beasts and Water	100
9.	Danger on the Loch	113
10.	The Water Horse	128
11.	At the Court of King Brude	144
12.	Magic and Miracles	160
13.	The Final Parting	176
	List of Characters	185

Court of King Brude

PICTLAND

Emchad's House
Dorcan's House

LOCH
NESS

Nesan's House

LÍOS
MÒR

IONA

DUN
ADD

DALRIADA

IRELAND

CHAPTER 1

Kidnap!

It was a scream that woke Colman. A scream so full of fear that his body went rigid. He sat bolt upright in bed and the blankets and sheepskins that had been covering him fell to the side. He would feel the terror that he felt then on the back of his neck to the end of his days.

Rooted to the spot, he glanced around anxiously in the dim light for Deirdre, his sister, who usually slept beside him. She was nowhere to be seen. The peat fire which had been damped down for the night smouldered in the middle of the floor. For a split second all seemed normal. Then another scream filled the little hut. It was coming from outside. It was Deirdre who was screaming.

His anxiety for his sister overcame his own fright and Colman leapt for the door. Tearing aside the heavy skins which covered it he rushed out. Deirdre was standing in front of their hut, her eyes filled with fear, staring out along the rocky shore. Her mouth was wide open but

1

there was no sound coming from it now. Her hands were clutching desperately at her long dark plaits. Colman followed her gaze. In one terrible moment he understood the reason for her terror.

'Picts!' he gasped.

At the far end of the bay they could see a longboat coming in to land; the oars creaking as they manoeuvred in to the beach. There were perhaps a couple of dozen men in it – warriors – and the golden early morning sun glinted on the metal of their weapons. Most had bushy red hair and long beards and there was a lot of shouting.

'No!' cried Colman incredulously. Picts had killed their parents and would certainly not hesitate to do the same to them as well. They had no time to lose. He rushed over to Deirdre who was still standing, immobile and rigid, staring at the ship. She was taller than him but he grabbed her arms and shook her hard.

'Come on! Deirdre! We must make a run for it! They' ll have seen the smoke from our huts from the sea. They' ll be coming for us!' He started to pull her.

'It's no use!' she said pulling against him. 'It's no use! They'll get us just the same as they get everybody!'

'Don't be silly Deirdre,' shouted Colman, desperation taking hold of him. 'We can run! We can hide! We know places to go that they will never find…. Besides there's Cruithnechan too.'

'Cruithnechan!' She repeated the name and the mention of it stirred her from her stupor. 'We must get him out of here!' She started running towards another hut that stood a short distance from their own.

Cruithnechan was an aged priest who had agreed to foster the two young children of a powerful Irish chieftain. In return for teaching them to read and write, Fearghal, their father, provided the old man with food and clothing.

Then suddenly, when they had been with the old man for about two years, news came of a disaster so terrible that even now it was sometimes hard to believe. A raid in the middle of the night had been made by Picts from over the sea. Colman remembered the haggard old woman who had brought them the news; her clothing torn and soaked with mud from her journey, her eyes staring wildly and her head jerking from side to side the whole time from the shock of the slaughter she had just witnessed. No-one had been left alive in their parents' fort. The old woman herself had only survived because she had been left for dead by the raiders.

Cruithnechan had let the children stay on with him and Colman found it hard now to remember his old home. Deirdre had become 'mother' to them all. She it was who had changed his name from Colm to Colman or Little Colm. Poor Deirdre! If he had been little at that time, she would only have been fourteen years old then herself. Poor Cruithnechan too. It had been hard for him to suddenly have the complete responsibility for two young children.

Thinking of him jolted Colman back into action and he raced after his sister towards the old man's hut. The skin was already drawn from his doorway and sunlight streamed into it. The hut itself nestled beside some large rocks and was actually hidden from the boat so they had some trouble at first convincing him that there was indeed danger to flee.

'I am too old for this sort of thing, my children,' he protested looking up from his psalms, 'but you two go.' It was as if they had been suggesting a pleasant walk. They refused to leave without him.

'Come on, Father Cruithnechan!' cried Deirdre frantically, hauling at his arm, 'you must come with us.'

'Then I'm taking my books,' he answered stubbornly, glancing at a pile of hefty tomes hanging in a bag from the roof.

'I'll carry them!' said Colman quickly, and he fetched a large stool and hurriedly climbed up to unhook the precious bag. Meanwhile Deirdre was leading Cruithnechan out by the hand. She looked round towards the beach. They were still out of sight of the invaders. Perhaps those men would not come to this end of the beach. But it was an unlikely hope. Their house with its little trail of night time smoke must have been clearly visible from the sea. There weren't any other houses on this part of the land for miles on either side. She pointed to the rocky scrubland that lay behind them.

'Come on,' she urged in a low voice, 'we'll go this way. We'll find somewhere to hide until they leave.' Colman followed, concentrating on the rough stones beneath his feet. It was not easy ground to hurry over at the best of times and even less so carrying a bag that was a heavy weight for a boy of his eleven years or so. But he knew there was too much danger to complain.

For a while they ran in silence, the only sound to be heard was the gasp of their panting breath as they pushed themselves on and on. Suddenly they were stopped in their tracks by the terrifying sound of a man's mighty roar behind them The intruders had discovered their empty huts!

The shock made the three turn and run as they had never run before, last year's bracken sinking beneath their feet as they crashed through it.

They had left the shelter of the big rocks now and were pushing their way through the little wood that lay beyond. But it was more difficult here as they had to force a path through stiff branches still wet with last night's dew. As

4

Deirdre and the old man fought their way through them the twigs snapped back into Colman. His face smarted and his eyes stung from them but there was no time to think about it.

They came to a dip in the lie of the land where the trees dropped to a little stream. The three slithered down the wet slippery slope. At the bottom they turned upstream and, wading through the clear water, which was sparkling in the morning sunlight, they hurried towards a large boulder which was almost hidden by the overhanging branch of a tree covered in young green leaves.

'In here!' whispered Deirdre urgently and they sank thankfully into the lee of the rock tucking themselves in as well as they could under the leafy branch.

Colman's heart was thudding in his chest. As his breath quietened he was aware of his face hurting from all the twigs that had been whipped into it during that headlong rush. He touched it carefully with his fingers and winced at the pain. He was also aware of a dull ache on his shoulder where the strap of the bag of books that he had been carrying had been digging into his skin. He looked at Deirdre who was sitting gasping for breath beside him and was about to say something when she laid a warning hand on his leg and put a finger to her mouth.

He cocked his head straining for any sound of the boatmen. At first he could hear only the trickling of the stream as it rushed past over the pebbles. Then he heard distant shouting increasing rapidly in strength and fury. The men were indeed pursuing them. Their trail would be easy to follow at this time of day not only through the broken bracken stalks but from the broken spiders' webs they had disturbed on their way. Even the absence of dew-drops on the tree branches would indicate the route they had taken. Colman had often tracked Deirdre by that method on some of her lone walks when she had gone out to collect berries.

Loud shouting now brought him back to reality. He cringed back into the shelter of the rock, his head pressing hard into Deirdre's chest. He could hear her heart thumping and knew that his own was beating as loudly. He shut his eyes. He dared not look. A light hand on his shoulder made him jump. An involuntary gasp escaped from his lips as his eyes sprung open and his head turned. It was only Cruithnechan! The old man gave him a look as if to say, 'Be of good courage.'

Colman stared back at him blankly. How could he be so calm?

They could hear the men sliding down the bank into the stream. They could also hear what they were saying but could not understand a word. It was a strange tongue that the men were speaking. They must indeed be Picts from Scotland – the same ruthless kind of men who had slaughtered their parents and kinsmen and decimated their village. At all costs they must not find them.

The shouting stopped suddenly and there seemed to be a debate going on with everyone talking at once. Of course! The men would not be able to find their tracks now as they had walked upstream through the water. A glimmer of hope rose in Colman's mind and strengthened as the voices faded away into the distance. The men had gone the other way!

Cautiously he sat up and, after getting a nod from Deirdre, he raised himself carefully and peered over the rock. There seemed to be no sign of anyone. The band of pursuers must have gone down stream, perhaps expecting them to have made off back to the shore. Colman stood up in relief. For the moment they were safe and it was unlikely that the men would search this way again.

Probably they would return to the huts and ransack them, though there was little of value there except food.

Suddenly he noticed with horror that there was still a warrior sitting with his back to them on a rock a little way off. He was bending forward as if he were removing something from his foot, perhaps a thorn. Alarmed Colman made to sit quietly down again, but he had forgotten the satchel full of books. As he moved, it slipped from his shoulder and fell with a loud splash into the water. He ducked. They heard a shout, presumably from the man who had been sitting there.

'Quickly!' said Deirdre under her breath, 'They'll come back for us now! We must crawl up under this tree and climb the bank.'

Colman needed no second bidding. He scrambled on all fours quickly up the slope, pushing his way through the low-hanging branches. The ground was damp beneath him, sodden with the decaying leaves of last autumn and he was soon covered with mud.

So engrossed was he in getting away that he thought of nothing else until he reached the top. Collapsing breathlessly on the soft earth, he looked round. Panic-stricken, he saw that Cruithnechan was still at the spot where they had been and through the leaves he could see the old man bent over the books in the stream. He had not even tried to escape with them! Nearer him halfway up the slope was Deirdre. She too was looking at the scene below and he could see tears streaking through the dirt on her face.

'He wouldn't come!' she cried in explanation as she clambered up beside Colman.

She had scarcely reached him when they heard shouting below. They could make out Cruithnechan's sonorous voice asking the intruders to turn to Christ and take on His peaceful ways. This was followed by jeering and more shouting from the gathered boatmen. Then there was a sudden frightening silence in which both Deirdre and Colman heard a loud splash followed by men's laughter.

Colman found that he was crying now too.

'No!' he shouted and stood up ready to run back down the slope. Deirdre put out a hand and stopped him.

'Come on Colman.' she wept. 'We can't help him now. We must go before they catch up on us too.'

Colman was reluctant to move until he heard the crackle of branches and saw one of the warriors pushing his way towards them through the undergrowth from the stream. The man was still a good way below them and there was a fair possibility that the two of them could outrun the raiders, especially now that they had no Cruithnechan to slow them down.

But they had reckoned without fate. Just as they set off, Deirdre tripped over a tree root and fell headlong. When she tried to stand up again she found that she could only hold her weight on one foot.

'Go without me, Colman!' she said desperately waving him on. 'I can't stand!'

Colman was aghast.

'I can't leave you!' he cried back as he struggled to drag her to her feet. She shook him off angrily.

'Go Colman! If you can escape you will one day be able to get your revenge. If they catch us both we have no hope at all.'

He knew that she was right. He hugged her, the only mother figure that he could remember, until she pushed him off roughly.

'Go! Now!' she cried hoarsely.

Colman ran sobbing from her into the shelter of the nearby thicket. Once under the cover of the trees he stopped and looked back. Through his tears he could see

8

some men approaching Deirdre and heard more laughing. He buried his face in his hands and wept.

He was startled out of his misery on hearing a shriek of pain from his sister. He peered out to see one of the men trying to pull her up by her plaits and he was on the point of rushing back to do something to help when he noticed another taller man push his way through to the front of the group. This man walked with an air of authority but Colman's eyes were riveted to his evil looking face which was a deep purple colour above his orange beard. In one movement the newcomer cuffed, with such vigour, the man who was holding Deirdre's hair that he knocked him completely sideways. There was another outbreak of shouting and jeering and then he watched, with horror, the tall man lift Deirdre as if she were a sack of corn and throw her over his shoulder.

Colman crouched back into the undergrowth. Now the warriors had Deirdre they would probably come after him. But it seemed not. He watched as they turned, still laughing, down the bank again towards the river and the shore. The last he saw of his sister was her dark plaits swinging down behind the knees of the man who carried her.

For a while he sat not knowing what to do, not really caring. The shock of everything that had happened had left him completely numb. He sat staring straight ahead towards the point where he had seen his sister disappear from view.

After a while he realised that it was beginning to feel colder and a wind was getting up. He was still crouching and his legs were sore as he stood up and stretched them. What should he do now?

At length he started to wander back the way they had so hurriedly come in the morning. Then as he approached the stream, he suddenly remembered Cruithnechan. What

D. Crookes.

had happened to him?

He clambered down the slope towards the rock behind which they had sheltered. He could see Cruithnechan lying motionless at the edge of the stream beside where the books had fallen into the water. Hardly daring, Colman bent down and touched Cruithnechan's face with his hand. It was cold and covered with blood. It seemed that he had been struck by a rock. Colman took one step back and sat down on his haunches staring wretchedly at the hermit's body.

Suddenly he noticed a hand twitch. Was he imagining it? He lent forward and took hold of the hand. Cruithnechan squeezed his weakly. Colman could scarcely believe it. The old man was alive!

'Father! Father!' he cried. Cruithnechan opened his eyes.

'My son!' His voice trembled. He tried to raise himself but was too weak. Colman put an arm under his head and sat, silent, his tears running down unchecked on to the old man's face.

'Don't worry about me, son,' Cruithnechan continued, 'I've had my day. I'm ready for God.'

'No! Don't die! Don't die, Father!' sobbed Colman. Cruithnechan was looking round questioningly.

'Deirdre?' he asked. Colman could hardly speak the words.

'They... They've taken her with them,' he said. Cruithnechan moaned at the news and his eyes closed as his head sank back.

'Poor Deirdre! May God give her strength.' He opened his eyes again and looked straight up at Colman. His voice sounded strange as he spoke.

'You must be brave now, Colman. You are your father's son. I... I... have to go now. I am being called...' His eyes focused on something behind Colman and the boy, suddenly fearful, turned to see whom he was looking at. The warriors back again? But there was no-one to be seen. He turned back to Cruithnechan puzzled. The old man's eyes had glazed over. He felt the priest squeeze his hand weakly as he said faintly, 'Be strong! May God go with you!' Then the old body relaxed and became limp in his arms. Cruithnechan was dead.

'No, no, no!' he shouted at the top of his voice, mindless even though the warriors might hear him. He was past the crying stage now. Cruithnechan was right. He was his father's son and knew that somehow or other he would avenge his family.

Colman stood up slowly and spotted the books lying nearby. He picked them out of the water. The ink had run and most of the writing had washed away – Cruithnechan's life's work! He would avenge this also. There was one book which had fallen out of the bag and was caught in a cleft in the rock. It was still dry! Balancing precariously on the edge of the stream, Colman managed to retrieve it.

Tucking the book under his arm he decided to go back to the shore and see what the warriors were doing. He approached the huts with care but there seemed to be no sign of any men there. He looked along the beach. There was no-one there either, nor even any sign of their boat. Then he heard the sound of men's voices singing lustily, rhythmically, and he looked out to sea. There was the boat already well out from the land with the oarsmen pulling in time to their singing. He shaded his eyes with his hand. He could not see Deirdre but he knew she must be aboard. The tears started to flow again now as he suddenly felt terribly alone. He went back to the hut, flung himself down on the bed and cried until he could cry no more. Then he sat up exhausted and resolved. He knew what he would do. He was going to follow those men. He was going to rescue Deirdre.

Then he remembered Cruithnechan. Slowly he made his way back to the stream where the old man lay. He would have to bury him. He couldn't leave him to the wild animals. He shuddered at the thought.

Although Cruithnechan had not been a heavy man, it was a difficult job for a boy of Colman's size to drag his body back to the shelter of their enclosure. It took him a long time. Then, slowly, he prepared a grave. It was a rather shallow one but it was the best he could do and he found plenty of stones to place on top so that the old man should not be disturbed. When he was finished he said a prayer for Cruithnechan, and at the same time made a vow to avenge his death.

Then he got out the little boat that they kept down by the shore for fishing. It was beginning to get dark now but no matter; he would be able to steer by the stars just as easily as by day with the added bonus that no bigger boats would see him. He knew in which direction the land of the Picts lay for Cruithnechan had often told them, his wrinkled hand stretching out in a wide gesture towards the north. He'd known another Colm once, he had said to them, who had gone that way to the land of the Picts.

Colman wrapped the dry book of psalms that he had so carefully rescued, in a large piece of skin, tying it tightly with thongs. Tucking the parcel under his arm, he took a last long look at the grave. Then he closed the enclosure gate, walked down to the sea and climbed into the boat. It was going to be a bright starry night.

He began to row. Soon he would get the little sail raised. He remembered Cruithnechan's last words of blessing and knew that God would be with him.

CHAPTER 2

A Strange Shore

The night was not as dark as Colman had expected but the air became much colder when dusk fell. As he grew tired from rowing he hoisted the little sail, a piece of canvas tied to a stick on either side of the boat. Then it was that he noticed how chilly it had become and he huddled into his cloak which now seemed so thin.

As the boat reached the open sea, the coldness in the air was even more marked and he began to row again to keep warm. The little boat was a curragh constructed of hide tied round a light framework, and it skimmed along almost effortlessly.

By God's good grace the wind and currents seemed to be carrying the craft towards Pictland and Dalriada. Colman was sure that when morning came he would find himself near to the coastline for on a clear day land had been easily visible from their enclosure. He rowed for as long as he could but when his eyes would stay open no

14

longer, he wrapped himself in his cloak for a quick nap. The wind was in the right direction and it was blowing only lightly. He could risk sleeping. After the ardours of the day he fell asleep immediately while the little boat continued to bob on the swell of the sea.

He woke to find that a storm had arisen – it was the sudden violent movement of the boat that aroused him. From a gentle rocking lulling motion the boat began to leap and bounce on the waves. At first he could not think where he was, then it all came rushing back to him and he remembered the events that had led to this voyage. He held on tightly to the inner spars of his curragh as the spray crashed all around him. Dawn was beginning to break. He looked in vain for any sign of land but there was nothing to be seen in any direction except waves and greyness.

Clinging desperately to the boat, Colman decided he should perhaps take down the sail if he could manage to crawl over to it. Gingerly he made his way as the spray whipped across his face, and with cold, almost numb, hands he eventually untied the sail from one side. It lashed out into the air like a pennant and Colman could hear it cracking above the noise of the roaring waves around him. Before he could reach it the spar which had held up the remaining side snapped suddenly in two and sail and post went flying off into the distance. By now Colman was petrified and helpless. He could see that the little craft was filling with water. Feebly, with one hand, he tried to scoop the water back over the side while he clung on grimly with the other, but he could see that more water was coming in with each wave that broke over the boat than ever he could hope to bail out.

Eventually, when his hand was paralysed with the coldness of the water and he was exhausted with the effort, he gave up. And suddenly through his head came some of the stories that Cruithnechan had told them about the monks who went voyaging. This was just the kind of journey many wandering Irish monks would delight in, with a storm so violent that they could take no decisions for themselves but would have to trust to God where they would land. Colman had no option now either. What would be, would be. Briefly he wondered how many of those who 'wandered for God' had met a watery grave. Then a great wave came crashing down over the curragh. Colman felt himself lose his grip on the boat as he was washed away from it. Then he knew no more.

Diarmaid, a young monk, was walking along the shore. The white pebbly sand was in stark contrast to the thundery grey clouds which were now mercifully blowing away to the north. It had been a terrible storm, one of which they had not seen the like since the middle of winter. Sometimes, however, freak storms such as this did occur in late springtime.

The glories of nature were not lost on Diarmaid as he walked, but the main reason for his morning expedition was to look for any wood that might have been washed up on the tide. They used driftwood at the monastery for building as well as for fuel and it was a daily task to gather it.

He had not gone very far along the wide sandy expanse when he spotted something odd up in the tide-line. It was an upturned curragh.

'Oh me! What have we got here?' he asked out loud.

He hurried over in alarm, his thoughts racing. Was this the boat of any of their own monks journeying back from some far off shore? The nearer that he got to the sorry looking vessel, the more he was sure that if anyone had

16

D. Crookes.

been in it, he would not have survived such a storm. The sharp whiteness of broken jagged spars jutted out through the torn hide covering. He did not recognise the boat as one of their own and for a fleeting moment he thought it might have come perhaps from Mull across the Sound and been blown out to sea by the storm. Instinct however, told him that it could not be so, for the storm had been blowing from the south-west. This boat could only have come from one direction and that was Ireland.

As soon as he reached the curragh Diarmaid lifted it automatically to see if there was any thing or anyone trapped underneath, though as the torn and battered structure had suggested there was no-one. He looked up and down the tide-line for a sign of life but all he saw were great banks of seaweed that the waves had torn from the rocks and delivered to the shore. He sighed.

'Well, there will be lots of seaweed to enrich our land and plenty to burn as well, but I'll need help to gather it above the tide-line before the sea comes back for it.'

He returned to the boat and began to drag it across the white sand for a little way. It was sodden and heavy and left a wide deep furrow behind him. He left it carefully up in some rocks at the top of the beach and was about to head back to the monastery when he heard the strangest sound. It was one of those noises that is so slight and so unexpected that one wonders if one has heard it at all. He frowned and looked back towards the beach. It was then that he noticed that one of the large clumps of storm-driven seaweed was actually moving. It was so eerie that his first reaction was to run. He had heard many tales of sea monsters. But he peered back again from the safety of a large rock.

The pile of seaweed was motionless again. Perhaps it was his imagination? He stepped out firmly, putting all stories of sea monsters to the back of his mind. It might be a seal exhausted by the storm and washed up here in its helplessness. A baby seal possibly – the clump of seaweed wasn't that big. He kept his eyes riveted on it as he walked gingerly back. He was almost upon it when there was a high-pitched kind of groan and the seaweed moved again. He jumped in fright as he suddenly noticed a small human hand sticking out of the clump.

Dear God! There was someone inside there – someone who was alive!

Hastily he bent down and pulled the seaweed away as gently as he could.

'Mercy on us! It's just a lad!'

The boy was not stirring now and Diarmaid wondered if he was dead. Then to his relief he saw his eyelids flicker as the boy moaned again.

'There, there, laddie!' he soothed him. 'You're safe now. We'll soon have you somewhere warm and dry.' He picked the bedraggled boy up in his arms. and with the storm clouds behind him, he set off for the monastery.

Feidhlim was busy in the hospital brewing up herbs when he heard a great commotion outside. Drawing aside the door curtain, he looked out. Coming in his direction from the enclosure gate was a large crowd of monks and in the middle was Diarmaid. He was carrying some sort of bundle – probably something he had found on the beach. That young Diarmaid was always beachcombing. Then as he drew nearer, Feidhlim realised that the bundle was a person – a small person. He rushed out towards them

'Mercy me! What's happened? Who's this?' and then when he looked more closely, he pushed all the questions from his mind and began to act.

'Quickly, bring him in!' he ordered.

He ran ahead and drew back the door curtain to let Diarmaid through.

'Stay out here just now!' he commanded the others. 'I'll shout if we need any assistance.' He rushed in to help Diarmaid.

'Is he alive?' he asked quickly. Diarmaid nodded wearily. 'I think so. Just!'

'Oh you poor mite,' said Feidhlim as he felt the boy's hands and cheeks. 'We must warm him up! Put these blankets on him and help me to rub his hands. I'll see if they have any stones warming in the bakehouse oven that we could use.' Some of the monks who were still gathered round willingly ran the errand to the bakehouse. Then taking a ladle full of the herbal brew that he had been in the process of making when all this had happened, Feidhlim poured some of it into a bowl.

'It'll be too hot as yet but perhaps he will be able to drink it by the time it has cooled a little. Where did you find him, Diarmaid? Had he got caught out on the hill when the storm struck? And who is he? I don't recognise him.'

Diarmaid shook his head.

'I'm afraid I know nothing about him, but he is certainly not of this island. I found him lying down on the shore washed up with the seaweed and there was a curragh lying beside him. The storm blew up from the south-west but I don't see how anyone could have come all the way from Ireland and survived it.'

Feidhlim continued rubbing the boy's arms.

'Well hopefully we shall find out in due course. Look! I think he is looking pinker in the cheeks already.' They smiled at each other and at that moment two of the younger monks came staggering in with blanket bundles which were obviously of very great weight.

'Here are the stones, Father Feidhlim,' one of them gasped, 'they are rather hot. Cook recommended that you wrap them in cloths before you put them into his bed.'

'Right, thank you boys,' said Feidhlim, 'I have some cloths here – these will do the trick, I am sure.' Deftly, he picked up each stone from the blanket with a cloth and twisting it neatly round, slipped it into the bed beside the bedraggled traveller until there were two on each side of him and a couple at his feet as well. Then he raised the boy on his arm and gave him a few sips of the herbal brew before laying him gently down again.

'There!' he said, pleased with his effort. 'Now all we can do is watch and wait and hope – and pray. Off you all go! Perhaps some of you might go back down to the shore and see if there are signs of anyone else who might have been in the curragh with the boy. It's unlikely that one so young would be travelling on his own.'

Diarmaid and the two young monks who had brought the stones filed out obediently and left old Feidhlim keeping vigil over his sorry charge.

Night was beginning to fall by the time Colman opened his eyes. Where was he? He glanced anxiously around the dark room. In one corner there was a little rush lamp burning and by its flickering light he could make out the shape of an elderly man bending over what looked like a book.

'Cruithnechan!' he shouted out joyfully, relieved that the terrible happenings had only been a dream. The man turned. It was not Cruithnechan, but the light from the oil lamp revealed a friendly face that smiled.

'Aha!' he cried cheerfully. 'The Good Lord has granted you to stay with us after all!'

Colman was puzzled now.

21

'Where am I?' he asked. 'Who are you?'

The old man chuckled, pleased that his patient was taking such an interest in the things around him.

'You are in Eilean I, the isle of Iona.'

'And is that in Pictland?' asked Colman. He had to know.

'At the moment debatable,' said the monk lightheartedly. 'However this is the isle where the holy Colmcille has set up his monastery.

Colman had heard of Colmcille – Colm of the Church. The Colm of whom Cruithnechan had often spoken. Oh Cruithnechan! His face clouded over as he remembered the events that had made him leave his Irish home.

'What is your name my boy, and where do you come from?' asked Feidhlim gently. Colman told him. He told him too of the raiders, of how Cruithnechan had been killed and Deirdre taken prisoner. Then it all became too much for him. He turned over in the bed and began to cry – an uncontrollable sobbing which was a mixture of relief at having arrived at a safe haven, and of delayed shock at all that had happened to him. He felt strong arms round him.

'There, there son! That's it, you have a good cry. You'll feel the better for it.' Feidhlim held him tightly but all Colman could feel was the tossing of the wild sea where he had ridden out the storm. When he could cry no more the old man laid him back gently on the pillow.

'There now! You wait there and I'll get you some broth from the bakehouse. You need a bit of building up now, I dare say. You just stay where you are.' So saying, he disappeared from view out of the door.

Weak and in shock Colman lay back on the bed. He had certainly no strength left to be going anywhere even if he had wanted to. He looked wonderingly round the room. It was not very bright but the oil lamp gave out enough light for him to make out most things.

Beside the lamp was a dresser, and on it a row of small pots. Above it, from a length of rope, hung many bunches of dried plants. The floor itself was strewn with dried grasses and rushes. Glancing in the opposite direction Colman was surprised to see another three beds similar to the one in which he himself was. The two nearest him were empty but in the furthest away bed beside the far wall, lay a still, recumbent form. Even as he watched, the body moved with a low groan. It turned over and Colman saw a pair of bright twinkling eyes sunk in a hollow face. He stared at them. The face returned a toothless smile and then, seemingly tired with the effort of doing even that, dropped back exhausted on to the pillow. At that point Feidhlim came bustling in with a couple of steaming bowls.

'Now then, my boy! This should do the trick! Come on, sit up!'

Colman hauled himself up to a sitting position suddenly realising how sore and stiff he was. He took the bowl thankfully and cradled it in his hands, pleased at its warmth. He watched as Feidhlim took the other bowl to the far bed in the corner where he raised the old man carefully with one arm while he fed the hot drink to him with the other hand.

'Now then, Father Oran,' he said in the tone of one who is speaking slowly to a little child, 'we have a visitor in with us today.'

The old man gave the same toothless grin, his dark eyes winkling as before and he nodded feebly. Feidhlim turned to Colman in explanation.

'Father Oran was on this island when we arrived. No-one knows how long he had been living here. He is an old man and doesn't realise the passing of the years. We have taken him in and looked after him, as you can see, but he is not long for this world. He doesn't say anything now at all, just smiles and nods, except sometimes in his sleep when he cries out in some strange language.' Colman smiled acknowledgement of Feidhlim's explanation and the little old man in the bed nodded sagely, his bead-like eyes gleaming in the light from the oil lamp.

After a good night's sleep Colman felt a lot better and asked if he might get up. Feidhlim agreed and went to find some clothes for him to wear. He came back with a fair-sized bundle.

'Here we are! This is what our pupil monks wear.' There was a warm tunic of soft white wool and an over-tunic with a hood made of darker coarser cloth. Colman put everything on. He was beginning to feel a bit more like himself.

'May I go outside?'

'Yes, indeed you may, but stay within the enclosure meantime.'

Colman nodded and with a last sheepish smile at the old man in the bed he stepped through the doorskin and went outside.

Once out, he stood blinking for a moment or two until his eyes had become accustomed to the bright sunlight. He reckoned that it must be at least mid-day from the position of the sun. He looked around. He could see the enclosure wall surrounding him, a tall wooden stockade on a low mound of earth. Within it was a variety of little huts and through the doorway of many of them he could see monks sitting writing. It reminded him yet again of Cruithnechan and he turned away with a start and looked out beyond the stockade.

Behind him lay some rough higher ground and there

24

was a small hill immediately visible. In front of him was grassier ground as he looked down towards the shore and out over a stretch of turquoise green water. Across the water rose many higher hills, higher than any he had ever seen in his life before. Down by the shore, men dressed in the same clothes as himself appeared to be working on the land, bending over the earth as if planting something.

Just then a hand clapped him on the shoulder. He turned sharply and found a young monk with a merry grin on his face. He seemed not much older than himself.

'Hallo!' the monk cried in a friendly voice. 'I'm Diarmaid. It was I who found you yesterday down by the shore.' Realisation spread over Colman's face.

'My name's Colman,' he volunteered almost apologetically, feeling very much a stranger.

'Where are you from, Colman?' asked Diarmaid, 'and what is your family?'

'I come from the north coast of Ireland,' said Colman 'and my father was a chieftain there, Fearghal of the Fortress. However a few years ago he and my mother and the rest of my family were slaughtered by a tribe of Picts. Everyone was killed except myself and my sister Deirdre and the poor unfortunate woman who brought us the news, for we two weren't in the Fortress when the Picts came. At that time we were being fostered so that I could receive a fitting education for a chieftain's son. We stayed on with our Foster Father – until the attack this week…'

His voice hesitated and he faltered, remembering the terror that had struck them… and Deirdre… and Cruithnechan.

'Go on,' encouraged Diarmaid, 'tell me if you can what happened.'

Slowly and with difficulty Colman began to tell again the story of the Pictish attack and of the death of

25

Cruithnechan and of the capture of his sister. While he spoke tears ran unchecked down his face and as he continued the grim tale, Diarmaid was moved to tears also.

'So I set out to follow their ship and somehow win Deirdre back,' sobbed Colman, 'but I see now how futile an idea that was. They could be anywhere now… it's no use!'

'Wait!' interrupted Diarmaid sniffing back his own tears. 'Don't be so hasty. Colmcille may know something of these people. There isn't much he doesn't know and even less he can't find out. Don't give up hope yet.'

Colman wiped his eyes with the back of his hand.

'You think so? Where is he then, this Colmcille, and can he really find out anything? You'd need to be a magician to find out that sort of thing!'

Diarmaid smiled. 'He is a magician of sorts! They call him the 'Crane Cleric' because of the crane, the bird with magical powers. He'll be here soon and then you'll see. He's been away on a mission and we're expecting him back any day now. In fact that's partly why I was down by the shore yesterday,' he added, 'in case they too had got caught in that storm. So you can imagine my horror when I first saw your upturned craft. However, it's as well I was there or you might not have survived. Come and I'll show you my hut.'

With a light springy step he set off and Colman followed, the stiffness in his joints scarcely allowing him to keep up. Soon they came to a small wattle hut. Inside, it was very similar to the one that he and Deirdre had shared back home, but it was a good bit smaller. With a start he noticed a book hanging down from the roof. It was exactly like the one Cruithnechan had had. Diarmaid saw where he was looking and laughed

'Aha!' he cried gleefully. 'It didn't take long for you to

26

spot it! After I had delivered you to the hospital last night I went back to the shore and found that carefully wrapped in skins. I'm afraid the water has got in a little but I am hoping that if we leave it hanging for a day or two it will dry out and the damage may not be too bad.' He felt it lightly with his fingers to see how damp it still was. 'It is immaculately copied. Did you do it?' he asked.

Colman reached up and touched it reverently.

'No,' he said sadly, 'it was Cruithnechan's life's work and it was because of it that he died…'

Suddenly from somewhere outside the hut came an eerie sound.

'Ho – ho – o – o – o!' A strange calling which sounded far away and yet at the same time very near. Colman frowned.

'What's that…?'

Diarmaid was laughing. A look of complete pleasure spread all over his face.

'That,' he announced dramatically, 'is Father Colmcille! Come on!'

Without a backward glance at his new-found friend, Diarmaid ran headlong out of the hut. Colman followed as quickly as he was able. As he went, he was aware that everyone else was running too. By the time they had reached the shore a large crowd had gathered. They were all looking out over the water towards the further shore and, as he strained his own eyes, Colman could make out a little crowd on the other side. He found Diarmaid down beside the water busy pushing out a little boat and a couple of sturdy monks were clambering aboard.

'What's happening Diarmaid?'

Diarmaid looked up at him.

'We're getting a boat ready to go and collect Colmcille and the others from the shore of Mull. You can come too if you're prepared to help row.'

Colman nodded. He had already forgotten Feidhlim's instructions to stay within the enclosure and was now glad to have some role in the general excitement.

'Come on then! Jump in!'

CHAPTER 3

The Crane Cleric

As the little boat crossed the water Diarmaid explained, between oarstrokes, that Colmcille had been away in the island of Mull. He was hoping to contact the various Pictish tribes that lived there, to explain to them that his monks intended to live peacefully on Iona and would not threaten them.

'The Picts are a funny lot,' Diarmaid added. 'When we came here last year there were some Pictish Druids living on the island. Since Conall King of Dalriada had already promised Iona to us, Colmcille ordered them off. There were some nasty scenes I can tell you, as the Druids weren't at all pleased – but they went eventually, vowing all kinds of revenge.' He screwed up his nose. 'The snag is that although King Conall considers the island is his to give to us, it does not necessarily mean that the Picts are of the same mind. They seem to think that it is theirs.'

Colman felt his skin prickle at the mention of Picts and

a vision of a purple-faced red-haired sea warrior rose up in front of him.

Diarmaid was watching him and guessed what was going through his head.

'Actually, all the Picts we have encountered so far have been very peaceable – that is, apart from the Druids that were on Iona when we arrived. '

The boys were rowing along with the two other men. As he pulled, Colman could feel the stiffness in his body wearing off. The time seemed to pass quickly with the effort. It didn't seem long before the people they had just left had shrunk to about a quarter of their size, while the party on the shore of Mull grew in size with every stroke of the oars. Soon they had reached them and a couple of men waded out to the boat, tucking their robes up above their knees to avoid soaking them. The light craft bobbed alarmingly as the two climbed aboard.

Colman guessed at once which was Colmcille, for the taller of the two spoke as soon as he saw Colman and it was the same clear sonorous voice that they had heard calling when they had been in Diarmaid's hut.

'Well now, what have we here?' he asked, smiling curiously down at Colman. 'Is this a traveller from Ireland that I see before me with a look of loss and revenge in his face?'

Colman gazed back astonished into the kindly grey eyes that met his.

'But how did you guess?' he blurted out.

He heard Diarmaid chuckle beside him.

'Father Colmcille doesn't guess, Colman. He knows. In fact he knows just about everything there is to know. Didn't I tell you he is called Crane Cleric!'

Now it was Colmcille's turn to be amused. He clapped Diarmaid over the shoulder.

'And here is my most loyal follower!' he announced conspiratorially to Colman with a wink. 'I missed you on this journey, Diarmaid.'

'And did you secure Iona for us?' asked Diarmaid eagerly.

Colmcille laughed, a deep resonant laugh.

'Well, yes and no,' he said. 'For the meantime we are quite safe, and for the rest…? Well, we'll leave it in the good Lord's hands. Why are we sitting here? Come on! I see a crowd waiting for us over there.' He and his companion sat down in the bottom of the boat while the four rowers began to ply their way back to the other shore once more. After only a few strokes the others stopped rowing almost as one. Diarmaid put up the sail. Colman was surprised and rested on his oar to watch.

'But there is no wind,' he said.'

'You wait!' whispered Diarmaid.

He leaned over towards Colmcille who was apparently already dozing on the floor of the craft.

'Father, we are tired of rowing and I have put up the sail. Do you think there could be a wind?'

Colmcille opened his eyes and sat up looking around him. For a moment he ignored them all and seemed not to have even heard Diarmaid. Colman looked from one to the other. Even the two older rowers were looking expectantly towards their abbot.

Colmcille stood up and gazed around him almost as if he were sniffing the air.

'Yes,' he said eventually. 'I think there might just be.' He raised a hand over the water and mumbled something that Colman could not hear and then, just as suddenly, lay down without a further word and shut his eyes again. Colman, puzzled, glanced at Diarmaid. Diarmaid caught his eye and winking, licked his finger and held it up in the air.

31

'Come on Colman, you do it too.' Colman copied slowly. He wet his forefinger by dangling it over the side and held it up above his head. Nothing. Not a breath of wind today. It was strange after the storm of yesterday.

All of a sudden he felt a coldness on one side of his finger and the boat began to rock. A wind was getting up. Diarmaid, he saw, was sitting by the sail and it was filling. There was a smug smile on the boy's face. Colman's mouth fell open in surprise. He was not sure now what to think about Colmcille. Here was a man who not only could tell where a person came from at the first meeting but could also command the wind. It just was not possible. And yet he himself had seen it with his own eyes.

He came out of his reverie to notice that the monks on the shore of Iona were cheering as they saw the boat pick up speed in the wind.

Before long, and without any effort on their part, they were at the landing place. The crowd gathered round Colmcille and, tugging at his sleeves, accompanied him up to the enclosure. Colman stayed behind and was helping Diarmaid tie up the boat when he heard a strange sound.

'Tong! Tong! Tong!'

'What's that?' asked Colman.

Diarmaid smiled and grabbed his arm.

'It's a while since we've heard that sound. That is the great clanging of Colmcille's bell. It is time for prayers and if we don't hurry we shall be late. The two hurried up the track and found the rest gathered by the time they reached the enclosure.

'Usually we say our own prayers in our own huts,' whispered Diarmaid, 'but always if Colmcille has been away anywhere, we gather together at the council place to give special thanks that our holy family is together once more.

Colman listened attentively as the monks sang the

32

evening psalms. He knew most of them by heart for he had been well schooled by Cruithnechan but he had never heard them sung together by so many.

He glanced out over the deep green water of the Sound of Iona that they had just crossed. As they sang, he was bewildered by the beauty and the peace of the evening, in complete contrast to the turmoil that he had just been through. He thought of Cruithnechan who, too, would have been saying his evening psalms in his hut only a few days ago and now… He thought inevitably of Deirdre and, as Colmcille's crystal voice led them all in singing, he found he could not stop the tears from coursing down his cheeks.

Evening prayers were over and they all remained at the meeting place. Colman wiped the tears with the back of his sleeve and took stock of his surroundings. There must have been a good thirty monks of all shapes and sizes. They all looked somewhat similar with their tonsures, where each had the fore part of their heads completely shaved in front of their ears. All were gazing eagerly towards their beloved leader.

Colmcille, sitting on a large stone, smiled slowly round the little gathering and Colman was once more left with the feeling that those soft grey eyes were looking into the very depths of his soul. He wriggled uneasily.

'My brothers,' the abbot began, 'I need hardly tell you how pleased I am to be back once more among you. Baithene and I had an interesting journey through Mull,' and he smiled at the other monk who had been his companion in the boat. 'I have both good and bad news to tell you.

'The good news is that the neighbouring Pictish tribes that live on this side of the island seem not to be too worried by our presence here. They are a little concerned that our worship of the White Christ will annoy the gods that they worship but that at least gives us something to work on.

'The bad news is that the Druids that we turned off the island last year when we arrived have apparently gone to their High King, Brude, to seek his support to turn us off the island.'

'And does that mean that the Picts will come with their King in force to expel us from Iona?' asked a familiar voice, and Colman turned to see Feidhlim with a worried look on his face.

'It's possible, Feidhlim,' continued Colmcille sagely, 'though I don't suppose that a handful of men living peaceably on an island at the edge of his territory is going to cause him much concern unless he happened to be in the area anyway. However King Conall of Dalriada did say that he couldn't guarantee our safety and I think it's up to us to make some kind of move anyway towards this great High King.'

'You mean, to show him that there is nothing for the Druids to fear from Christianity,' piped up Diarmaid excitedly.

'No!' said the older man sternly, 'I mean to show him that Christianity is more powerful than their Druidism. He will not dare to do any harm to us once he knows that we are under the protection of the most powerful God that there is.'

There was a general rumbling of consent round the gathering.

'It will mean a rather more prolonged trip away from you all as soon as possible, I'm afraid. The High King of the Picts lives far to the north east but I am told that the journey isn't too difficult as there are plenty of rivers and lochs. Most of it can be done by boat and we can go to

King Conall and borrow one of his guides to lead us. However I intend to have a week or two here to rest and to see how everything is going, before setting off again.'

The faces of the monks, which had become crestfallen at the news of the re-departure of their beloved abbot, lifted again at the news that he would be with them for some days at least.

'Now then,' continued Colmcille, on a lighter note, 'let's see young Colman here. Come here my boy. '

Colman rose obediently and went up to him.

'How are you feeling now, Colman?' and again Colman had the feeling of being completely transparent to the other man. His mind was confused and he stuttered over an answer to the question. Colmcille smiled,

'I know,' he said, 'it is confusing. So much has happened to you in so short a time, but be assured that all things are in the hands of our great God. Even the storms which seem to bring nothing but destruction bring some good in their wake. They bring us mounds of seaweed to fertilise the land – and the last one brought us you!' His eyes were twinkling now. 'We are both Colms,' he continued. 'They call me Colmcille, Colm of the church, and you are Colman, Little Colm. We shall go well together. We must see what we are going to do with you.'

He turned to the rest of the company and said, 'The meeting is finished. You may all go in peace.'

The monks left quietly and in single file towards one of the larger huts which Diarmaid had told Colman was their eating hut.

'Now Little Colm,' announced Colmcille beaming down at him as he stood up and Colman blushed. It pleased him to share a name with this great man. 'You and Diarmaid come with me and we shall have a wander round the island before darkness falls, I want to see how the crops are doing and I want to tell Diarmaid everything that has happened since I saw him last.' Diarmaid grinned with pleasure. In fact, Colman realised, he had not stopped smiling since his beloved Colmcille had returned. Colmcille now addressed Baithene who was still hovering nearby.

'You, Baithene, must rest today, and tomorrow you can start to write down what happened to us on our travels.' Baithene nodded,

'Yes Colmcille, I am indeed weary today.'

The four of them wandered down from the meeting place to the eating hut where they had a sparse meal of bread and water. Then, having soon eaten, Colmcille set out with Colman and Diarmaid.

They set off in a southerly direction up and over a small hill. Colman was hard put at first to keep up with them, for Colmcille was a tall man and his swift strides demanded almost a trot from Diarmaid and a run from Colman himself and Colman's joints were still aching a bit from his sea voyage. Soon he found himself out of breath and Diarmaid noticing, dropped back and let Colmcille go ahead.

'Go on, you stay with him,' panted Colman, 'I can't keep up with this.'

'No, I'll wait for you.' grinned Diarmaid. 'Colmcille won't even notice that we're no longer with him until he reaches the hill at the end of the island and we'll catch up with him when he stops. He always comes this way when things are on his mind and he won't want to talk to either of us until he has got his own problems sorted out.'

'Oh?' said Colman. It had not occurred that a man who seemed so much in charge of himself and everything around him, should have problems too.

'Besides,' continued Diarmaid lightly, 'I'll be able to

36

point out where you came ashore if you want.' The two boys slowed to a walk and followed in a more leisurely fashion the fast disappearing figure ahead of them with its robes flapping in the breeze.

Before long, they came to a place where the land opened out wide in front of them. There were flowers of every colour imaginable everywhere.

'This is the machair,' said Diarmaid indicating it with a wide sweep of his arm. 'Over there... and there... and there,' he pointed, 'you can see our barley growing.' That was why I came over here yesterday, to see if there had been any storm damage.'

'And was there?' asked Colman looking at the bright green patches of stalks that Diarmaid was showing him. The other boy shook his head.

'No, we were lucky this time. Just as you were lucky too. Over there is where I found you.' and he pointed again. Colman looked at the sea and the rocks. He had been lucky but he shivered despite himself.

'Come on,' urged Diarmaid thinking his friend was cold, 'we go this way.' He began to stride out as the ground climbed gently from the flower scented machair and soon they were crossing rough moorland. The ground here was uneven under their feet and they had to keep their eyes down to avoid twisting their ankles in the clumps of coarse grass, bracken and heather. They passed a small loch with last year's bog cotton bobbing beside it and as they passed two ducks flew noisily into the air.

By the time the boys had caught up with Colmcille the day was well advanced. As Diarmaid had predicted the abbot was indeed sitting on the hill, silhouetted against the evening sun. When they arrived he was gazing out to sea. Now he turned and seeing them smiled, starting out of his thoughts.

'My goodness, my sons! ' he said, 'I had forgotten all about you! Come here and sit down beside me.'

They did as they were told.

'The monks call this hill Càrn Cùl ri Eirinn, the Cairn of One's Back to Ireland,' Colmcille explained to Colman, 'because although Ireland is out there, you can not see it as it is so far away. You are therefore bound to turn away from it to the land you are on, and in, and part of. Strictly speaking the land you came from and this are joined as one by this sea. One day, though, this sea will separate the two. Then, in that day, there will be two countries speaking different languages and a lot of blood will be shed. But there will always be a shared history. That can never be taken away or denied. But, dear me! I am getting carried away with myself. How about you, Colman? Feidhlim told me that you were in a bad way yesterday.'

Colman looked at the kindly face. He felt that the older man already knew his innermost feelings but he said,

'I'm much better today, thank you Father...' and trailed off. What more was there to say that could ever be put into words – how he felt confused and bewildered at the sudden turn of events that had overtaken him, how he could not believe that his beloved teacher Cruithnechan was dead even though he had buried him with his own hands, how he longed more than anything to see his dear sister Deirdre again and feared against all his hopes that she too might be dead... if not at the hands of those pirates, perhaps even in the throes of the storm that he himself had survived, miraculously it seemed? How could he express in words that he longed most of all to be away from this strange land with people he did not know, kind though they had been, to be able to shut his eyes, and when he opened them, to find himself back in their little hut on the sea-shore in Ireland with Deirdre cooking over the warming fire and Cruithnechan chanting his psalms in the morning sun…?

Despite what Colmcille had said Colman searched the horizon eagerly for any sight of the land that he knew as home but there was nothing to be seen. He was right. Here one had to decide to turn away from Ireland and accept that you were in another country. He turned away from the sea and towards Colmcille who was watching him carefully.

'You've had a lot of terrible things happening to you, Colman,' he said gently. 'Many people would say you should forget about it all, forget everything that has happened and start a new life. From now on I want you to consider Iona as your own home. But I want you to tell me everything about the life you had, no matter how difficult, because I think it will help you to share the burden of sorrow… You were the son of a nobleman, were you not?'

Colman nodded again.

'My father was Fearghal of the Fortress… and the fortress we lived in was thought to be completely secure… but it wasn't. Picts from this land mounted an attack and killed all of our tribe…' He stopped, tears welling in his eyes.

'But you escaped,' prompted Colmcille softly. Colman shook his head.

'No. Deirdre and I were fostered out at the time with Cruithnechan, an old priest who was teaching us both…'

'Not Cruithnechan of the Green Sward?' interrupted Colmcille startled. An anxious frown furrowed his tonsured forehead.

'The same,' said Colman simply, not noticing the sudden deep concern of his listener, 'but we ourselves were attacked the other day and they took Deirdre with

39

them and they killed Cruithnechan…'

'No! No! I don't want to hear this!' shouted Colmcille aloud, standing up suddenly and angrily, and Diarmaid sprang up too, startled at this outburst.

Colman stared, totally bemused. First the holy Colmcille asked him to tell all about the terrible events; now he was shouting at him to stop!

He cowered at the monk's ranting, then noticed with surprise that Colmcille himself was crying now, openly and with seeming grief. He turned to Diarmaid who, though obviously distressed at the change in his master, could only shrug back with a woeful look on his face. He did not know what had caused the change.

After a while Colmcille stopped crying and, pulling himself to his full height, stretched out his hands to the skies,

'A curse on the wicked men who did this evil deed! May those who murdered my beloved Cruithnechan so mercilessly be themselves killed in some horrible manner!'

'What is it, Master?' said a timid Diarmaid beside him, once it seemed clear that the holy man was not going to say any more. Colmcille turned slowly to them both,

'Cruithnechan of the Green Sward was my teacher too, Colman, when I was a young lad. Some of my fondest memories are of that dear man and I owe him so much of what I now know. He must have been a very old man and did not deserve such an end. A curse on all those scoundrels! Tell me, did they kill your sister too?'

'That's what I don't know!' said Colman plaintively, 'She was alive when they took her but they were rough men and laughing evilly. There's no knowing what they might have done with her but I will not forget the one who carried her as long as I live.'

'Oh?' queried Colmcille, 'in what way?'

'Because although his hair was long and red like the other men he had purple skin over half his face.'

'Perhaps coloured for battle?' suggested Diarmaid. Colman didn't know, but Colmcille did. He sank back down again shaking his head.

'Things are more complicated than I feared. I have indeed heard of that man and that only the other day when I was in Mull. It was, I'm sure, none other than Broichan the Purple, the chief Druid of King Brude of the Picts. It was some of his friends that we chased off this island when we arrived and he it is who will be going to Brude to lay claim to Iona and the right to attack and murder our monks. This puts things in a different perspective. Our trip to the High King Brude is now a matter of the greatest urgency. I had hoped to rest here for a while before setting out again, but if Broichan the Purple is ahead of us on the road there is no time to lose. We must reach King Brude without delay.'

He stood up and set off back to the enclosure as absent-mindedly as he had come, leaving the two puzzled boys trotting in his wake. Colman was unsure whether he should be glad that there was some hope of Deirdre again or worried because she seemed to be in the grips of a most powerful and ruthless man with goodness knows what magical means at his disposal.

The boys reached the enclosure, panting and out of breath. There was no sign of Colmcille and indeed there were very few monks to be seen.

'It is the hour of nightfall,' said Diarmaid as if in answer to Colman's unspoken question. 'I must leave you and go and say my own prayers in my own hut. It's part of our rule.' Colman smiled.

'Of course, Diarmaid.' He was wondering what he would do next when he heard the familiar voice of

Feidhlim behind him,

'Ah! There you are Colman! What on earth have you been doing running all over the island, and you just recovering from death's door?' He was shaking his head. 'I don't know what the younger generation is coming to these days. I told you to keep within the enclosure. You ought to be conserving your strength. The holy Colmcille is a good man to be sure but sometimes he doesn't always think. I don't know, really I don't! Come away in to the infirmary out of the cold night air.' And he went ahead of Colman into the building, muttering all the while.

Inside, a small fire had been lit and it was really quite cosy. In the corner the old man was tossing a bit and mumbling to himself.

'Poor old Oran,' said Feidhlim stoking the fire with a stick, 'He's not too well tonight.'

'What's he saying' asked Colman unable to make it out.

'Oh, I don't know. I just chat away to him. I think it's the Pictish tongue. So Colmcille says, any way.'

Feidhlim gave Colman some broth and bread and soon, with a full stomach and the heat of the fire, he felt quite sleepy.

'You must go to bed now I think,' said Feidhlim, 'you've had a long day, rowing boats and running around the island like a madman, but we'll say no more about it!'

Colman needed no second bidding. He climbed on to his bed and fell asleep immediately, too tired to think even for a moment about his past or his future. Iona was his home now and tomorrow would be another day.

CHAPTER 4

Omens of Doom.

The next morning dawned bright and sunny. For a moment Colman thought he was back at home as he watched the sunlight glinting in through the doorskin. Then he remembered..

Hearing a strange whispering, he turned over in his bed to see Feidhlim and Colmcille standing with grave faces beside Oran.

Feidhlim looked up at the movement.

'Ah! Colman, you are awake.' He came over to Colman's bedside. 'How do you feel today?'

'I feel fine' answered Colman, 'but Oran? Is there something wrong?'

'Indeed yes,' sighed Feidhlim glancing back to where Colmcille now knelt praying earnestly beside the old man's bed. After a short time the abbot stood up giving him a pat on the shoulder. He came over to the other two.

'Hello, my Little Colm,' he smiled and Colman felt

43

engulfed by the warmth of his greeting. 'How are you this morning?'

Suddenly shy before the concern of the abbot, Colman could only stammer that he felt well. Colmcille nodded genially and went outside with Feidhlim. Colman heard them talking together in low voices as they stood in the sun on the doorstep. Then he could hear Colmcille leaving. Feidhlim came bustling back in.

'May I get up?' asked Colman.

'Of course,' replied Feidhlim. 'I'm afraid Oran will die today. He is so weak but Father Colmcille says that we must pray for him and wants us to take him out to our morning prayers.'

'Will that be where we had them last night?' asked Colman.

'No, that was the meeting place. This morning they will be at the open area – beside where we are building the new chapel. Some of the brothers will be coming in shortly to carry him there. You may go over with them if you like.'

Soon a group of younger monks appeared with a pallet and Colman was delighted to see that Diarmaid, his friend of the day before, was among them. The two boys grinned at each other briefly before the serious task of easing the old man gently on to the pallet began. Illness had wasted his body and Colman could see that the monks had no difficulty in carrying their burden as he followed them into the bright sunlight. As they wended their way towards the half-built chapel other monks left their huts and joined the procession. By the time they reached the place most of the community were present.

Colman could see Colmcille's head above the others even before he heard the sound of his bell ringing to call them all to prayer. He pushed his way to the front of the gathering and saw that they had laid Oran on his pallet in the lee of the half-finished chapel wall, for shelter from the sharp breeze that was blowing. The young monks who had carried him, including Diarmaid, stood beside him.

The abbot intoned a psalm and the company joined fervently with him in the singing. Perhaps if Colman had known the tune and had been singing too, things might have turned out differently. As it was he spent the time looking all around him – at the monks absorbed completely in their praise, at the deathly form of Oran on the pallet with the four bearers at each corner, and at the noble figure of Colmcille singing lustily – when all at once he noticed that the back wall of the chapel was shaking. So unexpected and slight was the movement that at first he thought it was his imagination. Then the wall was still again and he looked around at the faces of the others. They were all singing as before and no-one else seemed to have noticed anything out of the ordinary. He looked back at the wall and again he saw a definite trembling.

Colman jumped forward towards the small group beside the chapel with a shout just as the whole wall rocked and began to collapse towards them. The four pallet bearers, after what seemed like an age, reached hurriedly and desperately forwards to pull the pallet with Oran on it out of the way. Colmcille too took a step towards the wall when he saw what was happening. But it was too late. Diarmaid and one of the other bearers were flung to the ground by the falling rocks although the other two escaped unharmed. And as the tumbling masonry came to a standstill a white horse stood revealed on the other side. It had obviously been rubbing itself on the half-finished stonework and that had been enough to topple the wall. It got as much of a shock as anyone and set off at a gallop as fast as it could go in the other direction.

Colmcille was down on his knees tearing frantically at a pile of stones which had landed on top of the pallet and the sickly Oran. Colman rushed forward to join him with the rest of the monks. It didn't take long to uncover the old man but it was clear that the slim hold he had had on life was finally gone.

Colmcille sat back on his heels.

'He's dead,' he said simply, stating the fact. A new wave of shock ran through the community. Then Colman looked round and saw Diarmaid's motionless legs sticking out from under the pile of stones and began desperately to pull off the rocks which covered his friend. With relief he heard a groan and then Diarmaid sat up seemingly none the worse for being covered in rubble, apart from a graze on his forehead, but the other bearer who had also been caught under the wall found that his leg was very painful and that he could not even stand.

Colmcille took charge, asking some of the monks to carry the young monk with the sore leg back to the infirmary.

'We will leave poor Oran here meantime,' he added. 'We will have to bury him sooner than we thought, though not that much sooner, I suppose. He was ready to leave this world anyway.'

Colman accompanied Diarmaid back to the infirmary where Feidhlim put some liniment on his graze.

'You're lucky to have got off so lightly,' said the old monk, 'but you're going to have a real shiner there tomorow.'

They left Feidhlim dressing the other monk's leg. It was, they feared, broken, but Feidhlim had a way with such things and there was every chance that given time it would be better.

Colman and Diarmaid wandered around the enclosure.

They found the old horse that had caused all the commotion placidly eating grass.

'What will happen to him?' asked Colman.

'Her,' corrected Diarmaid. 'Nothing. She is Colmcille's own pet. He got her as a foal – a present from the very first Pictish chief that he converted to Christianity. To look at her now you'd never think that she had just killed someone.'

'Of course it was just an accident,' a loud voice boomed out behind them. They jumped, turning to see the tall figure of Colmcille. 'Besides,' he continued, 'Oran was nearing the end of this life any way and if the walls of the chapel were unstable it is probably better in the long run that we find out about it now rather than when the building is roofed and full of people.

'Is it indeed true Father, as they say, that every new building demands a human sacrifice?' asked Diarmaid.

Colmcille was suddenly angry. 'Who's been telling you such things? Of course not! That's pure druidic superstition. The White Christ that we follow does not demand such heathen sacrifices.'

His vehemence led Colman to suspect that he still half believed in human sacrifice himself. And later that day when they buried the body of Oran within the walls of the new chapel Colman confided his suspicions to Diarmaid.

'Just what I was thinking myself,' agreed Diarmaid. 'Why bury Oran here when there is a perfectly good burial ground already?'

Colmcille, who always seemed to appear at the least expected moment, overheard this remark too.

'Look you two ' he said impatiently, 'you may be right. Perhaps there always remains within us all a need to follow the old ways, but I do also need a saintly man to whom the chapel may be dedicated and Oran was saintly enough.

Besides, he was here in Iona before us and the first to die since our community arrived on this island. It seems fitting that we bury him in the new chapel. In years to come who knows but that the name of Oran will be remembered long after the story of his death is forgotten.' Colmcille winked at them. 'And you will see too that everyone here will be pleased and nobody compromised.'

He was right. Colman gazed round at the faces at the funeral service that they held later that afternoon and there was little sign of mourning. That it was a fitting end for so holy a man seemed to be the underlying emotion.

'And,' said Feidhlim to them later that night, 'many of the older monks were relieved that the old proprieties had been observed regarding a sacrifice for a new building without any untoward bloodshed.

Colmcille now became restless and agitated and a feeling of unease spread throughout the community. There seemed to be an evil presence among them which the death of Oran had only emphasised. After the funeral the abbot spoke to Diarmaid and Colman again.

'Tomorrow I must leave for the court of King Brude,' he said abruptly, 'There is evil afoot, I can sense it, and the sooner I see Brude and get to the bottom of it the better. Do you think you two boys will be able to cope with such a journey?'

'You mean we can come with you this time?' asked Diarmaid excitedly, scarcely believing his luck.

Colmcille laughed to see his excitement. 'Of course! I shall need you to look after me for it is a long trip. And if we catch up with Broichan the Purple perhaps Colman would like to be with us too in case there is any trace of his sister.'

'I'd like to catch hold of that man even if Deirdre is no

longer with him,' said Colman boldly and noticed Colmcille looking at him with a concerned frown.

'I hope you will not plan anything stupid,' said Colmcille, ' if I let you come.'

Colman pursed his lips tightly. It was more important to him than anything that he find out what had happened to his sister. Now here was a chance to catch up with the very man who had captured her. He had to go, and he would have agreed to anything to have that opportunity.

'No, of course not,' he said reluctantly.

They set off at first light the following morning. The sun was only just beginning to shows signs of rising over the horizon, as a warm golden glow filled the lower half of the blue sky. It was quite calm.

'It won't be like this for long,' said Diarmaid to Colman as everyone prepared to launch the two boats that they were taking on their journey.

They were a motley bunch. In addition to the two boys there were quite a few of the younger monks. They had been picked for their strength and would do most of the rowing and the carrying. It was not possible to sail their boats all the way to King Brude's palace and where the boats could not be sailed they would have to be carried. Diarmaid introduced Colman to a monk called Machar and another called Lugne. It was agreed that Baithene would go in one boat and Colmcille in the other.

'First,' announced Colmcille as they finally pushed off from the landing place to the waves and shouts of farewell from those of the community who were remaining behind, 'we must go to the court of King Conall of Dalriada. He will provide us with a guide, for he often sends messengers to King Brude. We also need an interpreter, for while the Picts may have some words of our

50

Gaelic speech, and I indeed have a few of theirs that I learned from my old teacher, we need to be sure of being clearly understood if our mission is not to be wasted.'

The men rowed the boat out a bit and then began to hoist the sails.

'But there isn't any wind,' said Colman to Diarmaid. 'We're not going to get anywhere!'

Diarmaid smiled and merely said 'You'll see. Do you not remember the other day when we went over to Mull?'

No sooner were the sails up than a wind began to blow from the west – at first just gently and then quite strongly, so that soon they were skimming along, only slowing to change tack.

Colman was amazed. 'I don't believe it,' he said incredulously. 'Where did the wind come from and how did it suddenly spring up just as they had raised the sail? It's magic.'

'No,' laughed Diarmaid, 'merely Colmcille, the Crane Cleric who has the strange power of being able to summon up the wind he wants whenever he wants. Some believe the power comes to him because he is so close to the good Lord and his creation. You watch him now.'

Colman turned to look at Colmcille who was sitting at the front of the boat, seemingly oblivious to the fine spray that was falling over him. His face was rapt with joy and he seemed to be looking at something beyond him. Occasionally Colman had seen that very same sort of look on the face of Cruithnechan.

'What's he seeing?' asked Colman intrigued.

'Who knows? He never says, but he always seems to have more vitality after such a time and with it a deeper peace… if you understand me.'

Colman could. He had discovered that with Cruithnechan too. Remembering Cruithnechan he began to think again about Deirdre, and yet he dared not think too much in case she should be already dead. He stretched a hand out over the side so that the tips of his fingers might dabble in the water. It was lovely and cool.

'Beware! There are monsters in this sea,' said Diarmaid behind him, 'just waiting to grab any one who dares to trespass on their territory.' Colman withdrew his hand quickly, looking round at the same time to see if this was another one of his jokes, but Diarmaid's face showed genuine concern.

'What kind of monsters?' he asked in awe.

'No one really knows,' said Diarmaid, 'those who have met one at close hand have never been seen again to tell their tale. We only have vague accounts from those who have seen their companions pulled, struggling, from their boats into the deep. One thing is certain though. The monsters are very, very big.' He stretched his arms out as widely as he could to give some indication of size.

Colman felt scared but did not dare to show it. What use would it be if Deirdre were alive and he was swallowed up by a monster before he ever got to her? Then he remembered Colmcille. Surely if he could control the wind he could also cope with monsters and he asked Diarmaid if that were so.

'You're catching on fast,' replied his friend, 'Yes! he can subdue monsters and even halt ordinary wild animals such as boars in their tracks. Humans too seem to fall quickly under his spell, though perhaps that is because they know that he has authority as a prince of the great Ui Neill.'

Colman had heard of the Ui Neill, the people of Niall, who were descended from the mighty Niall of the Nine Hostages one of the most famous heroes of history. To be a prince of that people was to be of noble blood indeed. He looked with fresh eyes of admiration at the tall man at the prow of the boat. His blood was far more royal than anyone of the line of Fearghal of the Fortress.

By this time they had long since left Iona behind and were skirting along the shore of a larger land.

'This is the island of Mull,' said Diarmaid, and Colman looked at the rocks and the steep craggy hillside. Ahead of them a blue grey land appeared, becoming ever clearer the nearer they drew.

Colman sat dreaming lulled by the gentle heaving of the waves. Suddenly he started out of his trance to find that Diarmaid was no longer by his side. He looked around for him and saw him up at the front of the boat with Colmcille and the two were deep in conversation.

'How he dotes on the abbot!' said Colman to himself out loud.

'Aye,' agreed a monk beside him, and Colman looked round in surprise to see Machar, unaware that he had uttered his thoughts aloud.

'Aye,' repeated Machar, 'Diarmaid is Colmcille's favourite, no doubt about it. Nor is there anything that the young lad wouldn't do for him. The life goes out of him any time the master is away and doesn't take him with him. Aye indeed…' and he sucked in his breath in a way that Colman had noticed many of the monks did when anything serious was under discussion.

Then he saw that Diarmaid was making his way back down towards him, his face glowing.

'Guess what?' he said when he was back sitting beside Colman. 'We're nearly there already. See! That's where we're heading, over there!' He pointed enthusiastically towards land that lay ahead of them, still too hazy to be made out yet in much detail. He could obviously hardly contain his excitement.

Colman was bemused.

'So?' he said, irritated by Diarmaid's excitement and to be honest, a twinge of jealousy that Colmcille should favour the other boy more than him, if what Machar had said was true. 'This is only the start of the journey. There's no point in getting excited yet.'

'But there is!' replied Diarmaid. 'Colmcille's just been telling me all about the court of King Conall. A greater and finer court than even those of Tara. With banquets and feasting the like of which we have never seen in our lives before.'

'Well, maybe not you,' said Colman quickly, 'but remember my father was a prince and we had feasting as a matter of course at our fortress.' He was boasting now. In fact it had been so long ago that he could not remember his father's court but Deirdre had told him many things about it. 'In fact he...' He was suddenly cut off mid-conversation as Machar pointed out towards their left with a fearful cry.

'Father! Look! Look!'

Everyone looked. About two boat lengths away and keeping pace with their speed was the biggest and blackest bird that Colman had ever seen. It looked exactly like a crow but was easily bigger than an eagle. He shivered with fear. There was something very evil about it. A hush fell over the sailors. The bird seemed to be watching them intently. Both boats seemed to be in the shadow of the big bird and they felt chilly – whether from lack of sun, or fear, none of them knew even if they had had time to think about it.

'What is it?' whispered Colman to Diarmaid, scarcely daring to make even the slightest sound.

'It's Morrigan' replied his friend dropping his voice even lower as he spoke, as if afraid of dire consequences even for mentioning the name.

54

Colman gasped. He had indeed heard of Morrigan, the most powerful and dreaded goddess, omen of doom and disaster. Was their journey fated even from the very start? He looked towards Colmcille. Would he save them? Could he save them?

The abbot stood as before at the front of their boat. His face was drawn now and he looked worried. He stared straight ahead, ignoring the bird flying along beside him. There was a look of concentration on his face as if he were willing their boat to go faster, to reach their destination before the evil wiles of Morrigan could prevent them.

All of a sudden the wind got up. All eyes were riveted on the bird which began to wheel and turn as it was buffeted by the gusts. The sea became very rough indeed as the storm increased to gale force and Morrigan seemed no longer to be able to keep up with them. Clutching to the side of the boat very hard, and trying not to remember a similar storm that he had been in only a couple of days before, Colman watched the bird with ashen face. Her wings flapped helplessly as she tried to make headway and eventually, with a disgruntled squawk, she wheeled round and dropped back.

A cheer went up around the boats but Colmcille raised a hand for calm.

'We have won through this time, my brothers,' his clear voice rang out over the sound of the wind and waves but I fear that she will be back. Morrigan does not give up so easily.'

Ahead of them now they could see land fast approaching. Never had anyone been so glad to see it. Colman shivered with fear.

CHAPTER 5

A Royal Feast

As they drew into the shelter of the land the force of the storm slackened. Colman could see that they were entering the mouth of a river. Beyond it he could make out the shape of a large hill which seemed to have some kind of fort at the top. There was smoke rising from it.

'I think that is Dun Add,' said Diarmaid, 'which is where King Conall holds court. It is where we are heading for.'

Colman was impressed. It was indeed the sort of spectacular fort that he would have expected such a noble king to have, rising grandly as it did out of the flat land all around. What a good vantage point it must be for spotting enemy attacks! Whoever was on the look out today would surely already be well aware of their presence.

The monks lowered the sails and began to row. All seemed calm now and there was no sign at all of the evil bird.

Soon, however, the current of the river became too strong for their rowing and they would have to leave their boats and walk the rest of the way. It was clear that this was the normal procedure, for there was a shelter by the bank and a little jetty as well. As they approached, a small young stocky man came out of the shelter and shouted that he would look after their boats if they would draw them up on to the bank. There were one or two other boats there already, small ones mostly, but there was also a long wooden ship out at anchor in mid stream.

'That must be the King's,' said Diarmaid gasping at the size of it and Colman too was amazed. He had never been so close to such a big ship before but it reminded him of the sort of ship used by the raiders who had gone off with Deirdre and he shivered. Being the youngest, the two boys had to jump out and pull on the boat ropes to steer the boat in to the right place. They splashed into the water while the rest of the monks continued to row. The boats glided with a dull scrunch on to the land. Then everyone else jumped out, headed by Colmcille, who greeted the boatkeeper.

'Well now, Garbhan,' he cried, grabbing him by the shoulders, 'How goes it now? Did the winter treat you kindly?'

Garbhan was clearly delighted to see Colmcille.

'Fine, just fine,' he stammered. 'Have you come all the way from Iona today?'

'Yes indeed, not a bad journey,' replied Colmcille with an easy laugh that belied the terror they had all felt because of the big black bird that had accompanied them. But he changed the subject quickly. 'How is your King?'

'His Majesty is well, thank you. He will be delighted to see you. I will send up my daughter to give him word that you are here. The lookout will no doubt have already seen

57

you but King Conall will want to send down an escort when he knows it is you.'

Colmcille smiled.

'That would be most kind.'

The man gave a low whistle. A small child came out of the little shelter and ran towards him, her bare feet skipping happily on the ground as she came.

'Go child, and tell the King's guards that the abbot Colmcille has newly arrived from Iona.'

'Yes, father,' she said and skipped off lightly. Colmcille smiled. 'She will make a fine mother one day, Garbhan.'

'Yes,' replied Garbhan, 'she already is a mother to me since her own mother was killed by raiders last year.' He busied himself with the ropes of their boat, turning away rather rudely, Colman thought, from Colmcille who had only been making kindly comment. He did not notice the man's tearfilled eyes till later. Then he remembered his own mother, and Deirdre, who had been as a mother to him for so long. Now he had lost his sister too. Everything seemed always to come back to that!

'We shall set off, my brothers, and meet the King's escort on the way,' announced Colmcille with a backward glance at the sky, impatient to keep moving, and he started walking at once, after bidding goodbye to the boatman, along a well-trodden track that led in the general direction of the fort. Diarmaid and Colman tagged along behind him, almost at a run to keep up with their leader's long urgent strides, followed by the rest of the company. They were thankful at last to have a break from rowing and to rest their weary arms.

At such a brisk speed they approached the Fort quite quickly. To Colman it seemed a forbidding rock which grew immense as they drew near. It rose up starkly from the level plain around it like a watchful monster. They

58

were almost at it when a small party of warriors came running out, spears in hand. Colman gasped but Diarmaid whispered to him

'It's all right. Colmcille is a friend here. The warriors are for escort only.'

He was right. The little band came up to them and it appeared that their leader knew Colmcille already.

'Welcome back, Holy Colmcille! My uncle the King greets you and looks forward to speaking with you.'

Colmcille smiled.

'Greetings to you too, Eoghan. I trust that all goes well with you. What news since I was with you last?'

'Little indeed. It has been a hard winter as you know and there has been no chance to travel round the kingdoms. News from the islands in the north indicates that the lands there are engaged in some kind of warfare, but a small scouting party sent out to find out the truth of the tales has not yet returned.'

Colmcille shook his head.

'Yes, I heard those rumours too, when I was in Mull a short while ago. It is imperative that those islands learn to live with each other or the way will be open for the Picts to muster them together and attack Dun Add.' He kicked a stone thoughtfully with his foot. 'Is there any word from or of the Picts?'

'No. There has been no word since the beginning of winter. The snow will have kept them in their fortresses.' He laughed lightly.

'Anyway, come on in! King Conall will be glad to see you.'

They followed him up a path which grew increasingly steep as they came up to the grand entrance of the fort. Diarmaid and Colman were panting by the time they reached the great gate which was in a large natural cleft of the rock. This brought them into an enclosure where there were women pounding grain on one side and, on the other, washing clothes beside a well. Everywhere there seemed to be animals and little children and the noise and clamour suddenly seemed overwhelming.

This was the first time Colman had seen any women in this land. He looked around automatically for Deirdre. They all had long dark hair like her and had stopped in their work to gaze at the newcomers. Some of the smallest children had rushed behind their mothers' skirts while many of the older ones came clamouring around, tugging at Colmcille's cloak.

'Colmcille! Colmcille! You're back!' they cried and they shouted with delight all the way through the enclosure.

Eoghan led them on through to a further enclosure and here obviously the children were not allowed for they dropped back at the gate. To one side was a large building, circular in shape, made of turfs and to the other, countless smaller ones of varying sizes. It was to one of the larger of these that Eoghan now led his little party. There were two armed guards at the door who stood to attention as Eoghan approached. Eoghan turned to the little group.

'Wait here a minute.' He disappeared inside the building and in a few minutes was out again.

'You may go in,' he said. 'The King is ready for you.'

Colmcille had to stoop to enter for the door was quite low. Even Colman had to duck his head a little. The room was full of smoke from a turf fire which was burning in the middle of the floor and it seemed very dark after being outside. As they became accustomed to the darkness Colman saw a dark haired man sitting on a chair on the far side from the door. His face was scarred and there was a sullen look in his eyes, yet he seemed pleased to see them.

'Greetings, kinsman,' he said rising to greet Colmcille.

'Greetings to you too Conall,' replied their leader in his strong resonant voice, strangely muffled in the walls of the building.

'We are pleased to see you. What brings you this way? Not bad news, I hope.'

'I think not,' replied Colmcille, 'but in these days one can never be too sure.' And he went on to relate the incident with the Druids on Iona and what he had also learnt in Mull. 'So we come to ask for a guide from you and indeed to tell you our plan in case you can suggest any better way of our making a peaceful yet forcible approach to Brude.'

Conall threw back his head and laughed. A deep roar of a laugh it was and Colman jumped.

'You do me a great honour, Colmcille, and I thank you for the compliment, but when did either of us ever take the advice of the other?'

Colmcille smiled a slow smile. 'You're right Conall, and yet I know so little of Brude that I want to have every advantage when I meet him.'

'All I know is that he was brought up far from the Pictish lands in the country of the Britons so that in a way he is a stranger in his own country. That may perhaps be used to advantage? He is also very much under the sway of his Chief Druid, Broichan, who advises him in all matters. They say that it is Broichan who is the real ruler.'

'Broichan the Purple?' echoed Colmcille and Colman shivered and listened intently.

'Yes, indeed, the very same. A ruthless man by all accounts.'

Colmcille nodded. 'Indeed, I had heard on my recent trip to Mull that it is he who is the brains behind the might of the Pictish nation, a power-mad man who advises King Brude to seize any chance to add Dalriada to his realm.

You must beware of him making any inroads into your territory.'

'We are on our guard all the time,' said Conall in a peeved voice, feeling that perhaps some criticism was now being aimed at him.

'Hmm!' said Colmcille non-committally. Colman felt that the abbot did not have a very high opinion of the King's ability to guard his kingdom.

'How long will you stay at our court this time?' asked King Conall, changing the subject. 'You are of course welcome for any length of time.'

'We thank you, King Conall,' replied Colmcille, 'But we will journey on at daybreak. There is a lot at stake. We have a long way to go and much to accomplish. I shall worry, until I see King Brude, lest some of his warriors, and his Chief Druid in particular, should descend on Iona in our absence. Can you provide us with a guide?'

'Indeed! Young Garbhan at the boats is your man. He is fleet of foot and knows the way between here and the fortress of King Brude like the back of his hand. What's more, he is well travelled and can speak not only the language of the Picts with ease but also the British tongue in which King Brude himself was brought up. He will be an asset.'

'Colmcille nodded briefly. 'Thank you Conall. He will be more than we had looked for.'

Conall smiled.

'And now to this evening! To celebrate your arrival and your departure we must lay on a feast or this isn't the court of King Conall!' He shouted a few sharp orders to some of his men who were standing by and they left immediately to organise things.

He turned back to them. 'Now, Colmcille, I should like to speak with you alone if tonight is all you have here.

Perhaps the others would like to wander outside and view the fort?'

Taking the hint, the small band of monks left the dark hut. Colman and Diarmaid followed their urge to reach the very topmost point of the fort and they found a narrow path leading up through the rock to two summits. On one there was a lookout and he greeted them.

'Well, boys,' he said. 'So you are with the Holy Colmcille are you?'

They nodded. He seemed a friendly man, though very large and broad.

'And are you staying long here?'

'No sir,' Diarmaid was the first to find his voice, 'we leave tomorrow for the kingdom of the Picts and the fort of King Brude.'

The soldier's eyebrows rose in surprise.

'My! That's a fair way and a long and difficult journey. I did it myself once with a party of soldiers and it took us all our time to defend ourselves, both from the wild animals and also from the wild people along the way. If it weren't Colmcille who were with you, I would say you were completely mad even to consider it, but it is said that the good abbot has a strange power over both man and beast so perhaps...' His voice trailed off and he looked strangely at the boys.'

Colman and Diarmaid glanced at each other apprehensively. Beasts? Wild people? The reality of the dangers that they might have to face was suddenly brought home to them.

'What kind of beasts did you meet?' asked Colman cautiously.

'Oh well, we met all kinds.' The lookout soldier warmed to the subject now with a faraway look in his eye, as he remembered past exploits. 'There were boars – which

63

were all right if we were prepared for them. Then there were wolves – who kept clear as long as we were moving but came in close at nights. There were bears too – big and strong... we had to kill one and then its mother went completely berserk.' He pulled up the sleeve of his leather jerkin and they saw two long scars running the length of his forearm. 'That was what the baby did to me and I was lucky. The man next to me took on the mother and has never been seen since.'

Colman shivered, wishing now that they had not heard any of this. Diarmaid nudged him.

'Come on, let's look round a bit more.' They took their leave of the lookout and noticing the twinkle in his eye, Diarmaid wondered how much of the story he had been telling them had been true.

They worked their way along a ridge of the rock towards the other summit. As they went, they came upon a large footprint in the rock and a shallow basin hollowed out of the stone nearby. Diarmaid saw them first.

'What's this? ' he said, and was about to put his foot into the print when Colman shouted out in alarm.

'No!' and he leapt towards him and knocked him over. Diarmaid was annoyed at this sudden and unprovoked attack and as he fought back the two boys rolled over and over on the rock. When they were finally exhausted Diarmaid sat up, still cross.

'Well, what was all that for?' he said angrily.

'You obviously don't know,' replied Colman, panting after the tussle. 'We had footprints like that back in Ireland and it's the worst possible luck to stand in them. They are used to transfer the power of the ancestors to the new king. No-one else must ever, ever stand in the print but the rightful heir. I've heard of people who have done it and none of them has lived for long afterwards.'

'Gosh!' said Diarmaid, appreciating how close he had been to a terrible fate and unable to say anything more.

They sat in silence together, contemplating the enormity of the situation and gazing out over the wide plain in front of them.

'What's the basin for?' asked Diarmaid after a while.

'Oh, it's all part of the crowning ceremony too. It's for the blood of a newly slain pig. The new king is branded on the forehead with it. I think in the old days they used the blood of a human enemy.'

'Ugh!' said Diarmaid in disgust. 'Why did they do it?'

'Don't know exactly. Something to do with the old gods of the land, I think.'

'That's right,' a deep voice sounded out behind them.

'Colmcille' they cried delightedly in unison and stood up, dusting down their tunics after the fight.

'I hope that by the time that the next King of Dalriada is due to be crowned we might perform the ceremony in Iona, thus breaking away from the old gods and the blood ceremony. Unity is what's needed to keep a kingdom together, not power or force or spirits of the ancestors.'

'Who will the next king be?' asked Diarmaid.

'Eoghan is the heir elect,' said Colmcille, 'and I think he will make a better king than his uncle. He's got much more get up and go than Conall, but he is also prepared to negotiate if he can, rather than waste valuable lives fighting.' The abbot picked up a stone and tossed it between his hands. 'Mind you, there's none braver than Eoghan when it comes to battle. Many a tale's been told of his prowess in the field. He'll be a much more suitable king than his brother Aidan – a nice enough lad but too quiet. He'll never be a good commander or leader. Perhaps he will come one day and make his home with us in Iona. I sometimes get a strange feeling about him.' His voice

66

trailed off and for a while he drifted into his own thoughts. The boys didn't disturb him. After a little, he came to himself again and said, 'Well, I suppose that it's time we all said our psalms before the feast begins.' He looked up at the sky. 'The sun is sinking and it will soon be evening.'

'Which way do we go tomorrow?' asked Diarmaid, and Colmcille stretched his arm towards the north. 'If we were going on foot, we would go that way up the old road of the dead, past the cairns that you can just see there and follow on in that direction. However, as we are going by boat we travel to the west of that route. Tomorrow we stop at the Isle of Lìos Mòr, hopefully to receive hospitality from my dear friend Moluag, and then from there on we are entirely in the hands of Garbhan of the Boats.' He smiled at their worried faces. 'Don't worry though. Everything will be all right. We are under the protection of the greatest Guide of all.'

His confidence was infectious and the boys could not but feel brighter. The trip was going to be an adventure after all. They skipped behind Colmcille as he made his way back down to the main courtyard. Here the monks gathered to sing their psalms, joined by some of the local inhabitants and watched by a good many more. Colman spotted some little children peering through a wicker fence at their singing and was at once both pleased and proud to be part of Colmcille's company. Suddenly he felt he belonged. If he didn't find Deirdre on this journey he would make his home in Iona. He would join the band of monks at Colmcille's monastery. He began to concentrate hard on the psalm singing in a determined attempt to blank out the possibility that he might never find Deirdre.

By the time the psalms were sung, preparations were

under way in earnest for the feast. A pig had been slain and now hung over a roaring fire at one side of the court-yard. Diarmaid and Colman went over to watch. A small lad, not much younger than themselves, was sitting turning the animal every so often. He smiled shyly at them.

'Do you go everywhere with Colmcille?' he asked in admiration.

'Nearly,' replied Diarmaid, 'it just depends where he is going and for what reason. Sometimes he just likes to be alone. But mostly if he takes anyone, he takes me.' Colman was aware of a touch of boasting coming into Diarmaid's voice. And again he felt a pang of jealousy. He knew of course that Diarmaid was Colmcille's favourite, just as he himself had once been Cruithnechan's. Tears sprang involuntarily to his eyes as he remembered the old man and he wandered off, casually he hoped, so that no-one would notice him trying hard to think of something pleas-ant or happy to take his mind off things. Oblivious of where he was going in his downcast state, he bumped almost straight into Colmcille.

'Colman!' he said in surprise, 'where are you going.' The mellow concerned voice was too much for Colman and he burst into tears.

'What is the matter, Colman?' A firm arm clutched him round the shoulders and the security made Colman blurt out, 'It's Cruithnechan… and Deirdre and… and… everything.' He let the tears run freely now. The arm clutched him even more firmly.

'Yes indeed, you poor boy. You have a heavy burden to bear. It may not ease the sorrow but you must remember that Cruithnechan is now in heaven, and as for Deirdre there is still a good hope that we may find her. However such burdens are not made any the easier for being tired and hungry and you are both. Come now ! Dry your eyes and let us go into the big hall. The King is preparing a feast and it will be a feast not only of food, but also of story and song such as I expect you have never heard before. I guarantee that it will lighten your heart.'

They went down together to the hall, joined by Diarmaid on the way. Tables had been set out in a rough circle and the monks were all bidden to their places. Ale and bread there was in plenty, as well as the roast pig. Colman noticed that Colmcille did not have any of the meat.

'Does he not like it?' he asked Diarmaid. Diarmaid shrugged.

'He has never eaten meat as far as I know. He feels animals are too much creatures of God but he lets us eat meat on special occasions, especially when it would be rude to do otherwise, as now. King Conall already knows about Colmcille and will not be offended if he doesn't join in fully in the feast.'

Colmcille had been right about the feast not only being food. While they were eating and long after they had had their fill, bards with their songs and storytellers with their tales told of the brave adventures and deeds of King Conall and of his forbears before him. A whole new world was opened up to Colman; a whole new country with its own stories of monsters and fairies, even though some of the stories about the older ancestors he already knew, for this people had come long ago, before the memory of anyone now living, to this land from his own country of Ireland. Monsters and ghouls mixed with kings and princes as the bards sang and Colman listened with alternating horror and admiration to the tales that were unfolded – tales of mist and mountain, of magic and mystery – so that he went to bed with his head reeling, and thoughts of his sister at the very outer edges of his mind, just as Colmcille had predicted.

Tomorrow they would be setting off towards those very hills and those very monsters and he could hardly contain his excitement.

CHAPTER 6

Lìos Mòr

They made an early start the next day. Ahead of them they had a long journey by sea and they wanted to reach the Isle of Lìos Mòr before nightfall. They said their farewells to the King and set off with their guide, Garbhan of the Boats, who was pleased to be included in the expedition. His brother would look after his young daughter and the boats in his absence, and he himself did not seem over-sorry to leave either. They loaded a large bag of presents from King Conall for King Brude and pushed off.

They were no sooner away from the land when a breeze got up, which turned steadily into a fresh wind blowing them in exactly the direction that they wished to go. Colman was no longer surprised though he gazed long and hard at the straight figure of Colmcille in the front of the boat and wondered how it was done.

Out into the open sea they had soon lost sight of the

rock of Dun Add. There was no rowing to be done because of the strength of the wind so they could all sit back and look around. They seemed to be heading right into those high mountains which had yesterday seemed so pale and far off. Now the same peaks and slopes loomed up darkly at them and seemed oppressive. Colman shivered and thought of Morrigan, but the skies were clear and he said nothing to Diarmaid.

After a while he slept, soothed by the rhythmic rocking of the boat and he woke when dusk was beginning to fall. The others showed him the island of Lìos Mòr – a long low island lying ahead of them in the twilight, like some enormous sleeping whale.

Colmcille guided them in to a little shingly beach where they jumped out and followed him up to the enclosure where the Holy Moluag lived with his monastic family. They had been noticed already despite the failing light, and a small party of monks was rushing out of the gate of the enclosure as they approached. At the head of them was a small slight man with a long flowing beard, in stark contrast to the baldness of his pate. Colmcille and he fell into each others arms immediately.

'Well, old fellow,' said Colmcille, when they had finished their greetings, 'how are things in this place?'

'Well enough, you old rascal,' replied the other, his face creased in smiles. 'It is indeed a strange time for travelling but no doubt you have your reasons. Did you come all the way from Iona today?'

'Not quite so far, Moluag,' replied Colmcille, 'Last night we were feasted at the court of King Conall and tomorrow we set out again bound for the court of King Brude.'

'Aha, so it's sucking up to kings that you are at,' replied Moluag with the tone of one who has just guessed a secret. 'And is it more islands that you are after? I dare say

72

Iona is really too small. It doesn't offer quite the same scope as we have here at Lìos Mòr.' He was chuckling now as he turned round to the audience of monks from Iona and gave an exaggerated wink.

Colmcille merely smiled at his friend.

'The size of an island is measured by its hospitality.'

'Ha,' laughed Moluag, throwing his head back and the long white beard danced in the night air like a little waterfall. 'Well spoken, my friend, well spoken! Come in to our enclosure and you will see that the Lìos Mòr, the Great Garth, is aptly named, for its hospitality is second to none…'

'Excepting, of course, that of Iona,' said Colmcille quickly, and Colman sensed a kind of congenial rivalry between the two men. Surely two such holy men of God were not concerned with trying to outdo each other in hospitality? It was kings and chieftains who did that to show their superiority… but abbots…? He followed the others into a large hut.

'This is the guest hut,' announced Moluag where you will all stay tonight – excepting yourself Colmcille. I have a spare hut where you may sleep.'

Colman looked round. The guest hut certainly looked bigger and grander than the one on Iona and there was sweet smelling fresh straw on the floor despite the fact that they would not have been expecting visitors. Moluag sent one of his monks to fetch some broth and some bread and while they were waiting he insisted that he wash all their feet. It was pleasant to be so pampered and Colman knew that for the abbot to wash their feet was the ultimate in hospitality.

'Colmcille will be seething' said Diarmaid softly to him as they sat waiting for their feet to be washed. 'Moluag is giving us the complete works. This hospitality will be hard

73

to beat and Colmcille hates to be beaten in anything.'

Colman glanced at Colmcille. It seemed that what Diarmaid had said was true. The abbot had a steely look on his face as he watched Moluag intent on his task.

Soon the foot washing was done and fully refreshed they sat down to their meal – a simple one compared to the standards of the night before but welcome none the less. Once they had eaten and were warmed, Moluag suggested that they join together in their evening psalm singing before they all turn in for the night and Colmcille brightened again and agreed wholeheartedly.

'That's because he knows that he can out-sing Moluag any day with that voice of his,' whispered Diarmaid to Colman. And that seemed to be true as well. Colmcille sang sweetly but loudly. As he sang, his face became rapt in the words and he seemed oblivious of the outside world. The point was made indeed but Colmcille was no longer caring.

The psalms were sung and a strange peace fell over the island. Looking out from the enclosure Colman and Diarmaid stood a while watching the moonlight rippling over the water and the stars twinkling above the high towering hills around them.

'Why does Moluag have a finger missing?' asked Colman, 'I noticed it when he was washing my feet.'

'There's a story to that, they say,' answered Diarmaid kicking a stone beneath his feet, ' whether it's true or not I don't know.

'About the time that Colmcille was looking for an island in which to set up a monastery, Moluag too was searching for one for himself. Both met up at the court of King Conall and it was agreed that the first to reach this island would be allowed to live on it as his own. King Conall gave them both a guide and the race was on.

74

'Well, you know Colmcille! He prayed, and the perfect wind got up right away, but he found out that he didn't have the monopoly on the wind that day. Moluag was more than a match for him and they sailed neck and neck down the firth towards this island. Perhaps Colmcille was a fraction ahead, who knows? However, apparently when they reached the island and Colmcille was on the point of jumping ashore, Moluag cut off his finger and threw it on to the beach ahead of his boat so that he could claim to be first on land.'

'Ugh! How could he?' said Colman pulling a face. Diarmaid shrugged,

'I did hear it said that the finger had already come off on the journey down when it had got stuck in an oar-hole, which seems the more likely. However Moluag certainly got the island and Colmcille had to look elsewhere, though he is more than pleased with Iona now.

'I think that Colmcille would have liked Lìos Mòr for its horses, for the Picts have always used this island for rearing and training their animals. It's a safe place for them to graze, free of the kind of wild beast that might attack them. And even though Moluag now lives on the island the Picts still keep their horses here as well. It's part of the deal whereby the Picts leave the monks in peace.'

Colman nodded. He had seen Colmcille's fondness for horses.

'Could Colmcille not have horses on Iona? There's plenty of room there too.'

'To tell the truth he's always been away ever since he arrived there so I don't suppose there has been much opportunity to think about horses. Perhaps when he has assurances from the Picts for his safety on Iona he will be able to turn his mind to things like that.

A hush descended over the enclosure as the monks of Moluag retired to their huts for the night. Only the slow swishing of the sea could be heard as it pounded out and in on the far rocks.

'Come on,' said Diarmaid 'I must go and see if Colmcille needs anything in his hut.' They walked in silence as far as the guest house and Colman went in by himself.

It was a large hut and several pallets were laid out side by side on the floor. The other monks in the party were already lying down in the dim light from a single lamp, and Colman found an empty pallet in a corner for himself. He did not know what time Diarmaid came to join him for he fell asleep immediately, still feeling as though he were tossing and turning on a boat.

The next morning turned out wild and wet and it would be a rough crossing for them to the end of the firth, even though they were quite sheltered by mountains on either side.

As soon as they had broken their fast, the little band of monks made their way down to the shore where they had left their boats. Moluag and Colmcille were already there, deep in conversation, and with them was a lanky youth whom Colman had noticed the night before. He had red hair of an intensity that he had only seen once before and that was on the tall man with the evil face who had taken his beloved Deirdre from him – Broichan the Purple. The boy had a simpering smile which made Colman feel uneasy, as if there were some kind of joke against him known only to the lad himself, but, since he had never met him before he knew that it could not be so. As Colman and Diarmaid reached the little beach, Colmcille turned to them.

'Ah! Boys! Just the very people we were speaking about.

I want you to meet Haldo,' and he indicated the gangly lad who smirked back at them. 'He is in fact a son of the High King Brude whom we go to see. He has been helping with the training of horses here in the Isle of Lìos Mòr but unfortunately he was kicked on the head by a lively stallion and has lost some of his senses, so that at times he seems to behave like a very young child despite his sixteen years. At other times he can become fierce and angry for no apparent reason, like a wild beast. He is no longer fit to be of any use here with the Picts' horses and although Moluag would gladly look after him, he feels that he might improve if he were back among his own people.' The boy continued to grin inanely at Colman and Diarmaid. 'And so, ' went on Colmcille 'we are going to take him back to the court of Brude and I want you two boys to look after him on the way.'

Colman's heart sank. Here they were on an adventure with Colmcille and hopefully going to find the where-abouts of his sister and now they were lumbered with this grinning youth.

Diarmaid asked 'Will he understand what we say to him?'

'Unlikely, I should say,' said Moluag and his eyes twin-kled in merriment and his silvery beard, cascading down his chest, shook as he laughed.

'Oh!' said Diarmaid. Colman could see he was wonder-ing how on earth they were going to look after Haldo if they couldn't communicate.

Moluag was speaking again, 'Unless, of course, you two boys can speak Pictish!' Now both he and Colmcille were laughing openly enjoying the joke together and Diarmaid and Colman were forced to smile.

Now Colmcille was speaking. 'Not to worry too much though, boys. We have another two travellers joining our party.' He indicated two older monks who were standing beside them. 'These are Comgall and Cainnech,' he continued, introducing them. 'They are old friends of mine from my youth and both have a smattering of Pictish and of course we have Garbhan too. They will all help with Haldo.'

Diarmaid gave the Pictish boy a smile. Haldo nodded back gapingly. Colman merely looked at him with some resentment, aware of the responsibility that Colmcille had imposed upon them. There was no time to do more, for Colmcille gave the signal for them all to scramble aboard. Once they were all in Moluag gave Garbhan some final instructions and waved them all goodbye. Haldo jumped up and down in his excitement and even with an arm apiece it was all Diarmaid and Colman could do to restrain him.

'Look, Haldo,' said Diarmaid impatiently, 'Will you please stand still or you'll have the whole boat upturned and us all in the water.' Haldo carried on jumping and waving wildly at Moluag shouting 'Oy! Oy!' at the top of his voice.

'Silly' said Colman to Diarmaid. 'He won't understand you. He's Pictish remember!'

'Right then!' replied Diarmaid. 'Will someone please give me the Pictish for 'stand still or else'…?'

'We won't need that.' A low voice behind them made them turn and even Haldo paused in his ranting to see who was so close to his back. It was Colmcille.

'Let go of him,' he ordered. Diarmaid and Colman surprised by his quiet authority, released Haldo's arms immediately. Colmcille took Haldo by the shoulders and turned him to face him.

'Now Haldo,' he said in his soft yet strong voice which commanded attention. 'I know about as much Pictish as you do Gaelic but if we are going to share a boat together, you and I, we are going to have to have some understanding between us.' He drew himself up to his full height and to Colman it seemed that he was towering above Haldo who was now gazing a little uncertainly up into the abbot's face. Colmcille drew the sign of the cross in the air above the boy.

'May the God of the wind and the waves, of the sun and the moon, of the Pict and the Gael alike, keep you in the calmness of His might.' Having said this he said to Diarmaid 'There, I think you'll find him easier to be with now.' And indeed Haldo was back to his original grinning self. Diarmaid pointed to the side of the little boat and Haldo went obediently with him to sit down while Colman followed wonderingly after.

By this time the Isle of Lìos Mòr was well away from them and they were heading up a long stretch of water with land, mostly mountains, on either side. They seemed almost impossibly high to Colman who had spent virtually all his life living by the seashore where the highest things were rocks and trees. He gaped in awe at the scenery.

Diarmaid meanwhile was making the best of a bad job and was pointing to various parts of his body, saying the name of it slowly and carefully to Haldo. Haldo soon picked this game up and began doing the same, making meaningless grunts for each part that he pointed to.

Eventually Diarmaid burst out laughing, which roused Colman from his mountain gazing.

'It's no good,' he giggled as he tried to attempt the noise Haldo was making, which came out like a sneeze as he pointed to his chin. He shouted over to Cainnech who was chatting quietly to someone at the back of the boat.

'Father Cainnech, how do you ever learn to speak Pictish?

79

'Oh it comes, it comes, my son,' the older man said smiling.

'All right then, let's hear you say "chin".'

'Atchoo' said Cainnech loudly with much concentration.

'Bless you brother!' came the deep tones of Colmcille's voice from the front of the boat where he sat without turning round.

Now everyone in the boat burst out laughing for all had been listening to the conversation which was being shouted from one end of the boat to the other. When Colmcille learned of his mistake he too, joined in the laughter. Perhaps Haldo was the most amused and pointing to his chin kept repeating 'Atchoo Atchoo', over and over again. He had found a joke that he could share with the company and was pleased to feel a part of it.

The sound of their laughing echoed across the water on the steep sides of the mountains which seemed indeed to be closing in on them as they travelled, for the channel of water on which they were sailing was becoming narrower all the time. Now, far from being sheltered by the mountains, it almost seemed as if the wind was intent on making mischief as it funnelled violently between the steep slopes.

The water became choppier the further they went and what had been a light drizzle turned into steady rain so that, even huddled beneath their cowls, they were soaked to the skin. Although no-one said a word they were all thinking about Morrigan and were glancing around timidly, fearful that they might see the form of the big black bird again. There was a sense of foreboding in the dim air.

'How much further do you think we have to go?' Colman asked Diarmaid. The journey seemed to be taking so long and he felt miserable in his wet clothes.

'Don't know,' he replied, ' but see, Garbhan is up at the front now speaking with Colmcille and pointing, so perhaps the end is in sight.'

'Why doesn't Colmcille make the weather better for us?' asked Colman 'He can do it. We've seen him.'

Diarmaid shrugged glumly in his wet clothes.

'Don't know that either. Just doesn't sometimes, that's all.'

Garbhan came down the boat towards them.

'We're in sight of the end of today's journey.' he announced. 'That's it there!' and he pointed to the shore.

At first Colman could not see anything but then very faintly through the mist and rain he noticed trails of smoke rising in front of some trees and as they grew ever nearer he could make out a group of little houses. It reminded him immediately of the two little huts by the Irish shore that he himself had once called home and in a moment of longing he forgot that home was now Iona.

'It must be a safe country here since they don't seem to have any fortifications round their village.' Diarmaid said, almost to himself, but Garbhan heard him.

'No indeed,' he said, 'It is no safer here than anywhere else these days. There are plenty of wild animals and also wild tribes of men who roam the forests, coming out to attack those who have a good living whenever times get hard. But the village keeps a constant lookout for these things and, if there is anything that the village guards cannot deal with the people are able to retreat with all their goods and animals into that building over there where they can be safe.'

'Where?' asked Colman and both he and Diarmaid were standing, peering at the shoreline, their hands shading their eyes. Haldo had got up too and stood beside them, though he obviously had not the slightest idea what they were doing.

'I see it!' cried Diarmaid pointing.

'Where? Where?' shouted Colman as Haldo began to jump about again, catching the excitement in their voices. Then he saw it. An enormous round tower. He gasped at its size.

'Did these men build that?' he asked, not really believing that anyone could build anything so big.

Garbhan shrugged. 'Who knows. I have stayed at this village often in the past and no-one there can remember when it was built. The broch they call it. Some say that it was constructed away back in the age of heroes when the great Finn travelled the land.'

'So! He was here too was he?' said Colman. He had heard of Finn the great warrior, perhaps the greatest warrior ever.

'There are stories of his exploits in these parts which the bards tell. You heard some of them the other night when you were at King Conall's feast,' continued Garbhan. 'All I know is that the people still use the tower though it's falling into disrepair a bit on the inside. '

There was a little crowd gathered on the pebbled shore to meet them as the two boats drew into the beach below the village. Both men and women stood with spears in their hands, eyeing them suspiciously until Garbhan jumped off the boat. Then there was a cheer as he was recognised and the spears were abandoned as the people rushed forward to greet him in the manner of a long lost friend.

After the initial delight had subsided, Garbhan said something to the crowd in a speech-like fashion and the strangers began to smile at the assembled boat party. There was a further exchange of words and then Garbhan turned back to the monks and said,

'As you may have gathered, the people welcome us and are pleased to give us their customary hospitality. Of course they have nowhere large enough to house us all together, so we shall be split up for tonight.'

They all walked together up to the village. Colman was beginning to shiver now in his damp clothes and was looking forward to the shelter of a house and perhaps a warm fire. When they reached the houses he was delighted to find that he was to share with Colmcille, Diarmaid, Haldo and Garbhan in the house of the man who seemed to be the village spokesman. Garbhan introduced them to each other, speaking in slow deliberate tones as he said each person's name.

Their host for the night was called Nesan the Crooked.

'Nesan,' explained Garbhan ' because he comes from a place near a river called Ness which is further north from here – in fact it is the way we shall be going. Crooked, because of the way he walks, as you can see. He was mauled by a boar as a youngster and was lucky to get away with his life.'

Nesan's wife was a bright kindly faced woman who fussed around them and kindled the small fire in the centre of the hut so that it was soon glowing with heat. She brought them all small cups with a drink in them and said something to Garbhan.

'We have been really honoured' he said, cradling the cup in his hands. 'This is the secret elixir of these parts, a potion that is said to restore health and to give long life to those who drink of it.'

Colman looked at his. It lay golden in his goblet but it didn't look anything special. Then he took a little sip. Immediately he could feel a warm glow spreading out from his throat, down through his whole body. He took

83

another sip and smiled as he realised that he no longer felt
wet and cold. As he continued sipping, the whole room
took on a rosy glow and in the smoke rising from the fire
he could see pictures – warrior heroes in shining clothes
and bards playing music. As he gazed open-mouthed at
the whole pageant, he felt himself just about to slip off
into a dreamland, when suddenly, he saw the form of
Deirdre rising from the fire towards him. If he stretched
he might just be able to catch hold of her as she passed.
He jumped up keeping his eyes firmly fixed on his sister.
His goblet fell unheeded to the rush-covered floor.

'Deirdre!' he cried, and as he stepped forward towards
her, he fell down in a faint.

CHAPTER 7

The Forest of Gloom

Whe he came to his senses again, Colman found the kindly face of Colmcille looking down at him. He could not remember much of what had happened except that he had seen Deirdre. He frowned, puzzled. Colmcille smiled.

'There now, Little Colm,' he said patting his hand gently. 'You're all right now.'

'But what happened? I saw Deirdre through the smoke of the fire. Where is she?' He could scarcely contain his excitement and panic in case she should slip away from him again just when he had found her. He sat bolt upright looking round the room for her but there was no sign.

Nesan, their host, gabbled something in Pictish to Garbhan who in turn whispered to Colmcille. Colman saw Diarmaid and Haldo at his other side, looking concerned. Colmcille spoke softly.

'I'm afraid it wasn't really Deirdre you saw, Little Colm…'

'But it was, it was, I saw her!' he protested.

Colmcille shook his head gravely.

'No my son. It was the drink that Nesan gave you that did it.'

Colman frowned.

'The drink…?'

'Yes. The heather ale. It's a potent brew made to a secret formula that only a few in these parts know how to make. It is a potion with strong healing powers and they say it can even give you eternal youth if you drink it regularly enough. It also gives you visions sometimes where you can see the past rolling before you and the future which is to come.' He smiled at Colman's incredulous expression. 'Don't worry. I too saw heroes from the past, and I expect everyone else did.' He glanced around and they were all nodding wistfully. 'Some people see these visions more clearly than others, so clearly that the people in them seem almost real. You saw Deirdre I take it.'

Colman nodded doubtfully.

'Yes, and she was as large and as solid as life.' He paused for a moment. 'Colmcille? Do you think that was a vision of the past or the future?'

'I don't know. But don't worry. Our times are in God's hands and what will be, will be.'

'What did you see, Father Colmcille?' interrupted Diarmaid.

The abbot lifted up his head and there was a shadow over his face.

'I saw my beautiful island of Iona as it was when we arrived. Then I saw many buildings on it and warriors burning and pillaging the buildings, and monks running in all directions trying to escape, but being cut down by swords. There was blood, lots of blood. Then nothing but cattle grazing.' There were tears running freely down his face now.

'I'm sorry Father, I didn't mean to…' said Diarmaid, wishing now that he hadn't asked, because of the distress he had caused his beloved Colmcille.

'It's all right, Diarmaid. I'm merely sorrowing for a passing phase in the life of Iona. There is joy too in that there will obviously be monks on Iona for some time to come. And though they may be chased away it will not be forever. For a while instead of monks' voices, there will be the lowing of cattle, but before the world comes to an end, Iona will be as it was.'

Diarmaid whistled. 'Gosh! Did you see all that in the smoke?'

Colmcille shook his head.

'No son. That's something else… call it an insight from God if you will.'

Suddenly Haldo started jumping up and down clutching his stomach and making a strange noise in his throat. Colmcille stood up concerned.

'What is the matter with him, I wonder? What's he saying Garbhan? Is he ill?'

Garbhan laughed.

'Perhaps he thinks so! We call it hunger! He is watching Nesan's wife pour out the broth.'

They all sat round the fire and gladly supped their broth noisily till they had drained their bowls. Colman was glad to feel full and warm again in the normal way without the strange accompanying visions. He lay back on a pile of bracken in the corner and listened as Colmcille, Garbhan and Nesan discussed the next part of their journey. At times Nesan was drawing with a stick on the earth of the floor while Colmcille and Garbhan watched intently. The in turn would ask questions and then Garbhan would take the stick and add something to the drawing. As he dozed, Colman heard the words 'wolves, bears and boar' and every so often when he looked over towards their faces which glowed red in the flickering firelight, he noticed Diarmaid sitting beside them looking very worried.

They all slept together that night huddled on the floor for warmth and they were indeed warm on a bed of dried heather and animal skins. But Colman shivered even in his cosiness as he snuggled in a thick black fur and could not forget the names of the wild animals that he had heard them speak that night.

In the morning they were up with the dawn. Today they would have to walk, for the current of the river was too strongly against them to risk using the boats. That meant that they would have to carry them and the going would be even more tricky.

Nesan was giving Colmcille and Garbhan some last minute instructions. Finally when all seemed to be arranged Colmcille turned to Garbhan and said,

'Ask Nesan how many cows he has.'

Nesan, surprised by the unexpected question, raised his eyebrows and answered briefly.

'He has five,' said Garbhan.

'My good man,' continued Colmcille, 'You have fed us and looked after us for a night stinting us for nothing. Your generous hospitality will not go unrewarded.'

Nesan was stammering now. He was very red in the face and becoming tongue-tied the more he tried to speak. Garbhan came to his rescue.

'I think he means to say that he wasn't looking for any reward. To entertain the great Colmcille was a pleasure and an honour in itself. He wishes he had more to offer in the way of hospitality.'

Colmcille smiled.

'Say nothing, good man. You may have only five cows just now but I tell you that they will increase to one hundred and five in number. And you will always have one hundred and five cows as long as you shall live no matter how many your generous nature feels inclined to give away. Nor, should greed overtake you – though that seems highly unlikely – will you be able to increase your stock beyond that number. And furthermore, both your children and grandchildren shall be blessed with fortune and all your descendants after that.'

Garbhan translated quickly. Nesan was gaping in incredulity now and stammering.

'He wants to know how this will be,' said Garbhan.

'The Good Lord above will organise all things,' said Colmcille briefly. He turned to go. 'And now for your hospitality we give you many thanks once again. Come let us join the rest of our party.'

The others were outside. When he realised that they were setting out again Haldo began to get excited and started to jump up and down. Colman watched as Colmcille went over to him and laid a hand on his forehead. Haldo was subdued immediately. He gazed into the older man's face with a momentary look of rapture on his own before the simpering smile returned, but he was no longer jumping. He came over to stand beside Colman and Diarmaid who were talking together.

'What was that I heard last night about wolves and bears, Diarmaid,' asked Colman.

Diarmaid's face was for once unusually grim.

'Nesan was telling us of the dangers that might lie ahead for us,' he said.

'But Colmcille can command the waves. What can a wild animal do that could be worse than the wrath of the sea?

Diarmaid shook his head slowly.

'The sea is an inanimate thing. Its force can be harnessed for good and Colmcille can do that. But wild animals can be filled with evil spirits and it can take a lot of force to reckon with them. Not only are there wild beasts but also wild men who have failed to be accepted in ordinary communities, usually because they are too violent, and these roam the wild country looking for whatever mischief they can find to do. Particularly, they will pounce on unwary travellers who might be carrying gold or treasure. What chance have such as we against such warriors? I can't see even Colmcille stand against such wildness. Can you?'

Colman ignored the grinning Haldo beside them.

'But you of all people, Diarmaid, know that Colmcille believes this journey to be the will of God. How can we perish if that is so?'

'I don't know but I do wish we were travelling all the way by boat. It's too scary having to go through the trees. Anything or anyone could jump out on us there without warning.'

Diarmaid looked up at the broch beside them, dwarfed by the high snow-capped hills behind that had yesterday been hidden from them in the rainy mists. Whoever had built that fortress knew what he was about in these wild mountainous parts. He admired the pluck of Nesan to live freely outside its walls, banking on having time to run for shelter if they should need it. Give me an island any day, thought Diarmaid. There at least you could see your enemy coming a good way off. No furtive skulking behind forest tree trunks.

They were sorry indeed to say good bye to Nesan the crooked. He and his family waved them out of sight which wasn't far, for the track that they were following led quickly into the forest.

Almost at once Colman felt creepy shivers down his back and with every crack of a twig that he heard in the trees on either side, he started and looked sharply in that direction. He, Diarmaid and Haldo kept up to the front of the party, close behind Colmcille and Garbhan. They were carrying the sails for the boats and, as the path seemed to be climbing upwards, it was very tiring.

Colman nearly jumped completely out of his skin when a thin scrawny man suddenly leapt out of the murk of the trees on to the path in front of Colmcille. Colmcille did not flinch. He stopped though.

'May the One True God be with you,' he said.

Colman peering round, could see that the man in front of them had a dirty face and a very lean look. His hollow eyes told of hunger. He began to gabble at them.

Colmcille turned to Garbhan.

'What is this man trying to tell us?'

'He is saying that he is a very poor hunter and that he is so bad at hunting that he is now too weak to roam the hills after the deer and other wild animals. He had heard that you had dealt generously with Nesan the Crooked and begs for alms for himself.' The man was by now kneeling on the ground in front of Colmcille still gabbling, looking up at Colmcille very now and again with a shifty look in his eye that Colman did not like or trust.

'News travels fast indeed!' said the abbot. 'And how is it that an able-bodied man like you cannot earn his own way in the world?'

Garbhan related this to the unfortunate man. The man straightened up at this and gave a low wolf-whistle between his teeth. Suddenly from all around them, rising as it were straight out of the bracken came about half a dozen scruffy solemn-looking children with dull flat eyes

gazing out of grubby faces. All looked thin and hungry, a look borne out by their lack of energy and expressionless faces. They hovered at the edge of the trees while a thin woman came and stood beside the man kneeling on the ground who said something further to Garbhan.

'This is the man's wife and family,' said Garbhan stating the obvious.

Colmcille frowned. He glanced round the ragged company that had sprung out of the trees.

'It is not right for an able-bodied man to beg in this fashion. Nevertheless, neither is it right for the whole family to suffer because of the inadequacy of its head. You!' he added, pointing to the man, 'Go into this wood and bring me as long and straight a branch as you can find!'

Garbhan translated, and the man got up slowly and went into the forest watched by the eyes of his family as well as those of the monks who were all curious to know what Colmcille was up to.

He vanished from sight, but shortly after there was a loud crack followed by another and the shifty man reappeared with a good sized stake. He held it out to Colmcille who took it, and borrowing a knife from Garbhan, began to sharpen it. All eyes were upon him as he pared the wood away, not least those of the beggar. Colman guessed that the poor man had been expecting perhaps a cow or two to be magicked out of the air. Certainly not a stake.

'There now!' said Colmcille giving a final flick to the point. He made the sign of the cross over it and handed it to the astonished man. 'Look after this stake and it will catch all manner of wild animals and fish. In fact you will never lack for food again in your household. But though it will kill wild animals it will never kill people or cattle. Take it and look after it well and make better use of your life.'

94

The man smiled as Garbhan explained and fell down on his knees once more, gabbling what was clearly thanks. Colmcille bent and lifted him upright.

'Go!' he said, 'and be happy!' He smiled as they all watched the ragged little party depart, slinking and merging back into the trees and bracken as noiselessly as they had come. The gaunt face of the man's wife stuck in Colman's memory. How thin she was! So many children to feed... and yet there was a youthfulness in that sorrowful face that reminded him of Deirdre. She could be a beggar too by now. Or worse! He shuddered to think of it. Diarmaid was asking Colmcille a question.

'What was the stick for, Father?'

'For catching wild animals to feed that poor unfortunate family of his.'

'But how?' queried Diarmaid. 'It was surely too thick to be a spear.'

'Indeed yes,' replied Colmcille. 'He doesn't have to do anything with it. Wherever he leaves it a wild animal will fall on it every time he has need of food... just so long as he continues to trust in its power.'

Diarmaid whistled between his teeth.

'So he's made for life!'

'It should work out that way but...' and the abbot shook his head, '... I don't know. Somehow I feel that he will not be able to handle even that.'

They shouldered their boats again and continued on their way. It was not easy going, being very steep in places, and both Colman and Diarmaid wished that they were back at sea again where the wind did most of the work.

There was a path but it was not well defined, and one needed to keep one's eyes constantly on it. Colman found himself at the same time drawn to look into the depths of the trees, expecting at any moment all manner of wild things, both man and beast, to spring out at them. When they stopped at a stream he confided his fears to Diarmaid and found that his friend felt the same way.

They continued walking during the afternoon and the air grew steadily heavier and more oppressive. Every noise they heard made them jump now and they had the feeling that they were being watched. The sky began to get very dark. Even the trees seemed to take a life of their own and were looming menacingly on every side, groaning and creaking as the band of monks passed, despite there being no wind.

Garbhan at the head of the party stopped.

'It's going to rain, Colmcille. I think we should stop here while we still have the shelter of the trees. Very soon the path will open out to the first of the lochs where we can use the boats.'

Colman shivered when he heard they were going to stop in among the trees. He felt uneasy and the forest around was unnerving, eerie. He felt suddenly shut in as if he were smothering. He wanted to get out, to go on, to reach the loch where they could feel the fresh breezes on their faces and breathe!

Colmcille was looking at the sky and deliberating.

'You're right, Garbhan. There is going to be a heavy downpour in a short while but I would like to get out of these woods as soon as possible, if we can. There is something menacing in the air that I can't quite place. There are many evil spirits living here on the look out for unwar travellers. If we stop now, I don't know if I should have the strength to cope with them.'

'Let us help!' It was Comgall and Cainnech, the two older monks who had joined them at the island of Lìs Mòr, who had kept to the rear of the column and ha walked most of the way so far in complete silence. 'Sure we three together will be match enough for any evil spirits that could possibly lay hold on us.'

Reluctantly Colmcille agreed.

'All right then. But just until this storm blows over. Then we must continue on our way and reach the loch before nightfall. Even the three of us together might not be stronger than the evil forces that lurk here in the hours of darkness.

They found a tree that had been blown down in a previous storm and sheltered in the lee of its roots with their boats upturned over them for extra protection.

The rain began suddenly, just when it seemed the air could not get any darker or heavier. Soon it was pounding on the bottom of the boats. Diarmaid, Colman and Haldo crouched down low, huddling together out of both fear and coldness.

Colmcille, looking as nervous as Colman had ever seen him, glanced back and forth uneasily. Slowly and deliberately he began to sing a psalm. At first his voice was low, unlike his usual strident sounds, but as Comgall and Cainnech joined in, he began to increase in strength and loudness until by the end of the psalm he was singing as lustily as he had been in his own Iona or even on Moluag's island of Lìos Mòr just a couple of days before.

As they finished singing the raindrops were beating down like little drumsticks on the boats. Colmcille stood up

'I must go and pray a while.' he said. Comgall opened his mouth to restrain him but Colman saw Cainnech lay a hand on Comgall's arm and shake his head.

'It would not do to try and keep him back,' he said once Colmcille had gone out into the storm. 'When he is troubled, he has to pray, and he has to be alone. He was always like that you will remember.'

'Have you known Colmcille a long time?' asked Colman, as much to take his mind off the weather and to reassure himself he was not alone, as out of curiosity.

Comgall looked at Cainnech and they smiled at each other.

'Yes child. We were all youths together back in Ireland. We learnt to read and write together. That's where Colmcille got his name. He was always going off by himself to pray. He hasn't changed. He was headstrong and independent then, as now!

There was a flash of lightning. It lit up the trees all around them and Colman could see gnarled and twisted shapes writhing and swinging on every side. He screamed involuntarily and was surprised to feel Haldo lay a reassuring hand on his arm. The last thing he could deal with just now was Haldo and his silly grinning.

He turned round and in the next awful flash he could see quite clearly that Haldo was not grinning. He was looking just as frightened as Colman felt, and his face lit up briefly in horror, was grotesque! A deep roll of thunder followed the flashes and in it a dark shape slipped under the boat. It was Colmcille back. They were safe!

But they were not.

'It's Morrigan!' whispered Colmcille under his breath to Comgall and Cainnech but there was a sudden lull in the noise of the storm as if even the elements feared that name and they all heard what he said with dread Morrigan, portent of doom and disaster, was with them still. They had not escaped her. Their journey was after all fated. Even the presence of Colmcille could not stop the inevitability of death where Morrigan was involved.

'What do you mean, Morrigan?' said Comgall out loud in a sort of irritable voice – the sort you use to speak to someone you suspect is making up stories.

For answer Colmcille merely turned and pointed away from him into the trees.

'Look!' he said simply, 'on the middle branch of that dead tree!'

They all looked where he indicated. At first all was blackness and then lit up in one awful flash of lightning was Morrigan herself looking bigger and more terrible than she had when they had seen her last.

As the lightning continued, each flash bounced off the enormous raven until it seemed almost metallic. The bird sat hunched against the rain, gazing steadily at them.

'Yes, perhaps I do see what you mean,' said Comgall less confidently now, but he was not one to let fear get the better of his common sense. 'Well what are we going to do about it? I mean we can't just sit here, can we?'

Colmcille gave a deep sigh.

'No,' he said slowly, wearily. 'I think we'll have to move on, storm or no storm. We can't risk being caught in the trees here after dark, not with Morrigan sitting there. We aren't far from the next loch, are we, Garbhan?'

Their guide shook his head. Poor man, thought Colman. He had maybe been this way a few times but from the whiteness of his face it would seem that he had never encountered a Goddess of Doom before. Keeping one eye on the black form huddled in the tree, they shouldered the boats and set off once more. The rain was still teeming down but none of them noticed it now.

CHAPTER 8

Wild Beasts and Water

They went slowly against the driving rain. Each step seemed to use up all the energy they had. Whenever they looked round, Morrigan the Raven was still following them. They never actually saw her fly, but each time they looked, she was sitting on a branch close behind them. The air was oppressive and the trees themselves seemed to be closing in on them. Colman felt panic rising in him. He wanted to run and run, to get away from everything, only he felt at the same time rooted to the spot.

Colmcille suggested that they sing psalms and hymns as they went and softly he led them in the singing. Gradually, as they sang, strength returned to them. Their voices became louder and they felt their feet grow lighter and the way easier. Looking round cautiously, Colman noticed that Morrigan was keeping further back now and he noticed also a quiet smile of triumph on the face of their leader.

Suddenly they were at the end of the loch and it

stretched out, a welcome expanse, in front of them. At the same moment the sun came out and the rain eased. They looked back. There was no sign of Morrigan now.

'We've done it,' shouted Colman and he, Diarmaid and Haldo jumped for joy.

'Yes,' added Colmcille 'for the meantime… but Morrigan does not give up that easily. She will be back. And we must be on our guard for her.'

They made the boats ready in the shortest time ever, boarding them and paddling up the loch as if their very lives depended on it – which in fact they felt might be the case. For a while they rowed to help speed the sails but as they tired and there was still no sign of Morrigan, they relaxed a bit and took a rest.

'Looks like we're safe,' Colmcille shouted to Baithene in the other boat. 'We can leave our boats in the power of God's wind now.' He turned to Garbhan 'How far can we go today and how far does this water stretch?'

'Well, it depends on the speed of the wind, of course, but I think we would be pushed to reach the end of this loch before nightfall. We might just do it but beyond it there is another stretch of forest to negotiate and from what you say, with that raven on our tail, it might be dangerous to be stuck there in the dark.'

'Indeed,' agreed Colmcille to Colman's relief. 'Well, let's go as far as we can and then camp by the lochside for the night. Then if trouble arises we can jump into the boats if need be.'

They continued sailing and for a while could sit back and survey the hills and trees around them from the safety of the boats. But all too soon it seemed, darkness began to fall.

At first it was just a grey soft light that transformed the menace of the trees on the surrounding shore and hills into something soft and dreamlike. Gradually, as it faded still further, it began to accentuate the darkness and gloom of those very same trees. They could see that they were nearly at the end of the loch and Garbhan pointed to the shore on their left

'It's a little bit flatter here,' he said, ' and we should see anything or anyone that approached.'

They pulled up the boats and made them into a shelter again. They were on a spur of land which had no trees on it and the wind was blowing straight across.

'You all try to sleep,' said Colmcille. 'I'll keep watch.'

'Not at all, Colmcille,' said Comgall quickly. 'We'll all take a turn. You need your rest as much as any of us.'

'No Comgall, not this time. I have things to think about. Sleep will not come to me anyway tonight.' ·

Comgall shrugged his shoulders at Cainnech.

'Always obstinate, eh? Age has not softened your stubbornness Colmcille. All right, have it your own way then.'

They made themselves as comfortable as they could, huddling under the boats. They were hungry for it had been a long and frightening day. They shared out what bread they had and then tried to settle down to sleep.

Colman could not. He found himself on the edge of the gathering and felt cold from the draught at his back. But it was the coldness of his thoughts that kept him wide awake. His ears, too, were pricked for the slightest sound that might indicate a return of Morrigan or indeed of the wild men and beasts that they had heard so much of.

Tired and despairing, he listened to the heavy breathing and the snores of the other monks. His eyes, accustomed to the dark, could just make out the shape of Diarmaid's face. It was thrown right back into Haldo's lap and his mouth was hanging wide open. He wished with all his heart that Deirdre was with him and then realising that it was no use wishing, he got up carefully and squeezed under the edge of the boat and went to look for Colmcille.

There was a perfect crescent moon over the loch and Colman could see the ripples in its reflection. Where was Colmcille? He didn't want to stray too far from the company of the others who, though sleeping, would still be of help should any wild thing attack him. He would look first down by the water.

He was heading down when, all of a sudden, he heard an almighty groan. He jumped. What was it? Whatever it was, it was coming from somewhere along the shore. Colmcille! Was he in trouble? He began to speed up his pace, steeling himself to rescue Colmcille from goodness only knows what. As he ran past a low outcrop of rock, something shot out and grabbed him from behind. He tried to scream but his mouth was covered, and the grip was so firm that he couldn't even struggle.

'Sssssh! Colman it's me!' The grasp relaxed and Colman turned to face Colmcille!

What on earth was going on?

Then he heard the strange groaning sound again behind him. It wasn't coming from Colmcille then!

Colmcille drew him gently by the arm behind a rock. He leant over Colman's ear.

'Watch,' he said pointing up the shoreline.

That indeed seemed to be where the groans and strange noises were originating. Colman peered. Then suddenly he caught sight of three, no four, big black shapes moving about at the edge of the water. He grasped Colmcille in fear. Was it some of the servants of the terrible Morrigan? In the moonlight he could see a smile on Colmcille's face as he shook his head and pointed back to the dark shapes on the beach.

One of them seemed to be bigger than the others and

the three smaller ones were bounding at it. The big one was making the groaning noises with the occasional deeper growl. The smaller ones were leaping everywhere now, sometimes on the bigger shape, sometimes on each other. They were a kind of animal but what kind? And why was Colmcille not afraid? It must be safe, for the abbot had been terrified at the sight of Morrigan.

They watched for a while from behind the rock as the shapes rolled around, growling, snarling and groaning. Sometimes they went running into the water and then came out, shaking themselves. Suddenly the biggest one seemed to stand up tall on its two back legs and sniff the air. It looked round tentatively in their direction. Colman froze and could feel Colmcille holding him still. Then the shapes went lumbering off into the darkness of the forest not far away from them.

'What were they?' whispered Colman once they had gone and a moment's wait proved that they were not coming back again.

'Bears,' said Colmcille smiling. 'It was a mother with her three cubs having a little fun together.'

'And are they not dangerous?' asked Colman.

'Yes, very!' replied the older man, 'but only if they are disturbed or attacked. There is probably no animal more dangerous than a mother bear with her young ones – for they are terribly strong – except perhaps some of the water monsters.'

Colman had heard of those too. Every loch had its monster. Colman glanced quickly out over the water but all was calm as it rippled naturally in the moonlight.

'Why are you not sleeping, my son?' Colmcille sat down on a rock at the top of the beach. Colman went over and sat beside him.

'I couldn't, Colmcille. I was cold and... and... too

many frightening things were going round and round in my mind.'

'You mean Morrigan?'

'Well yes, I suppose I do really. I just can't get her out of my mind.'

'She's like that. Tries to wear you down with the thought of death.' Colmcille's voice sounded grim. 'Death itself is nothing to worry about but the fear of it is something different. I expect she is making you think of Deirdre and death as one and the same thing.'

'Well, yes,' answered Colman, surprised that he should be able to pinpoint exactly what had been worrying him. Then he remembered what Diarmaid had said about the abbot when he had met Colmcille that first day, sailing across to Iona from the island of Mull. 'Father Colmcille doesn't guess. He knows just about everything there is to know.'

'Don't worry about her.' said Colmcille 'The good God made us all and is in all that is around us. Look at the beauty of that moon, of the water rippling in the night wind, the stars shining above us. His goodness is stronger than any evil there might be. Don't worry, Little Colm. Everything will work out for the best, I am sure.'

Colman shivered.

'Anyway, it is too cold for you out here. Go back to the others and try to get some sleep. We have a long way to go tomorrow and you will be weary enough by the end of the day without being tired to start with.'

'Are you not coming back to the boats too?' asked Colman. It felt so safe beside him.

'No, not yet,' replied Colmcille. 'I must pray awhile yet. There are many things at stake on this trip.'

Colman returned to the shelter of the boats. He crawled back into the place where he had been before. He had to smile when he saw Diarmaid and Haldo. They were in exactly the same position as they had been when he had left them and Diarmaid's mouth was still hanging wide open. He pulled his cloak around himself and curled up beside them.

In no time at all it was morning. Colman was woken by Diarmaid.

'Hey, stop that!' he cried, as his friend stretched a lazy foot right into his face. He pushed it away but it came back again and in no time at all they were rolling around in a friendly tussle while Haldo watched, grinning as usual.

'Right, come on boys,' said Comgall planting his staff between them. 'We are going now. That is, if we can find Colmcille.'

The boys jumped up, dusting themselves down hurriedly and Diarmaid gave Colman a friendly cuff on the head. Colman did not take him on again.

'I think I know where he is,' he said importantly. 'Will I just go and see?' He ran off in the direction he had gone the night before. In daylight it was not difficult to find the way back to the place among the rocks where they had watched the bears.

He rounded the corner where Colmcille had held him safe and there indeed was Colmcille, sitting just as he had left him with his back to him. He was about to shout out when he noticed that Colmcille was gazing up into the air and looking intently at what seemed to be a bright light. He stopped in his tracks and waited to see what would happen. The abbot was not only looking – he was listening too. The light came down closer to him – then suddenly vanished.

Colmcille sat back, looking very tired for a moment or two and then realising that he was not alone, he turned to Colman.

'You have come to fetch me because we are about to go.' His face relaxed into a smile at the look of surprise on Colman's face at his accurate guess. 'And I'll tell you more,' he added with a twinkle in his eye, 'I'll wager that it was old Comgall the Battleaxe that sent you. Come on then, let's go! I am ready and there is a lot to do.'

'What was that light I saw, Colmcille?' Colman asked straightaway.

The abbot looked at him carefully and did not answer him immediately. When he did, Colman noticed that his tone of voice was unusually serious.

'I will tell you, Colman. But I ask you to keep it a secret between us two.'

'Of course,' said Colman, wondering what could be so secret.

'The light you saw was an angel sent from heaven. It seems that there is an old man close to death ahead of us just off the trail and we must go and preach to him so that he may believe in the one God and be baptised before his death.' He sighed wearily. 'There is no time to lose. Come on.'

Colman quickened his pace to keep up with the abbot and was almost running by the time they reached the boats.

'Come on, Colmcille!' said Comgall 'The night is long gone and we must away. The day looks pleasanter and, so far, there is no sign of Morrigan. The faster we travel the better, as far as I'm concerned.'

They pushed the boats out into the loch and scrambled in. They had only a little way further to go before they would have to climb out again and head once more into the forest along the narrow path through the trees.

Colman was still wondering about the light he had seen with Colmcille and was longing to tell Diarmaid about it, but remembered that he had promised not to.

'You're very quiet this morning, Colman,' said Diarmaid. 'Isn't he, Haldo?'

Colman pursed his mouth, scared that he might just blurt out the very thing that he had promised to keep secret. Diarmaid was intrigued.

'You're not still holding it against me because I put my foot in your face this morning, are you?'

Colman shook his head. He was as resolved not to tell what he had seen as Diarmaid was determined to prise it out of him. He shared a secret with Colmcille that no-one else shared, not even Diarmaid, and he felt very special because of it.

Fortunately for Colman they reached the point where they had to get out of the boats again and carry them. The effort required to walk over the rough track made it difficult to carry on a conversation at the same time.

There was no sign of Morrigan so far that morning, although Colman noticed that from the front of the column where he was walking with Garbhan, Colmcille kept glancing back from time to time. They were clearly not free of that danger yet! The trees hemmed them in again and the feeling that they were being watched once more took hold of Colman.

Morrigan! With every bird that flew close to them, he looked up fearful and ready to duck or run. Though there were many, they saw no sign of the Raven Goddess herself.

'We're really into Pictish country now,' he overheard Garbhan telling Colmcille. 'And our lives are no longer as safe as they were. Some of these Pictish peoples can be nasty and assume any stranger to be an enemy.'

'You mean, act first, ask questions later,' said Colmcille.

'Exactly so,' replied Garbhan. 'If we meet any of them

we must all stand completely still. That is what they will least expect and that will hopefully give me enough time to explain our mission.'

After a while they came to a place where another loch stretched in front of them. Colmcille was beginning to look impatient and Colman assumed that it was because he was worried about the possibility of Morrigan following them.

As they launched the boats again, he urged them to hurry.

'We need a wind,' he said tetchily.

Almost at once, it seemed like magic, a breeze began to blow which increased to a strong wind just perfect for their needs.

It was a relief to be back on the water again. Without a path to follow, Colman had time to sit back and look at the steep forested slopes on either side of them.

'Are there monsters in those forests, do you suppose, Diarmaid?' he asked his friend.

'Certainly there are. There must be. And what could anything living in such dark forests be but evil?'

Colman shivered. He was, he realised now, both cold and hungry. They had not had much to eat on their journey and yet they had been travelling quite hard.

All at once they seemed to catch a cross-wind, and the boat took off in a kind of dervish dance, lurching and swaying this way and that, almost with a life of its own. Colman had been idly dreaming and thinking mainly of food. Now he sat bolt upright and clutched on to the sides. Looking across, he could see that the other boat in which Comgall and Cainnech were sailing with Baithene was being carried in a completely different direction. He saw Garbhan shout for Colmcille who was lying down in the bottom of their boat catching up on his lack of sleep the night before.

Colmcille sat up slowly. Then as he realised that they were taking in water fast, he sprang up and began to help the rest of them with baling.

There was shouting coming from the other boat and Colman looked up. It was Comgall.

'Never mind the baling, Colmcille ' he was shouting. 'We need more than that! Start praying!'

Colmcille frowned, but made his way to the prow of the tossing boat and stood unsteadily beside Garbhan who was frantically throwing out water with his cupped hands. Colman could see from Garbhan's face that he did not see much point in praying at this stage. Nevertheless Colmcille stood holding a hand steadily in the direction they wanted to go. His lips were moving but the sound of waves splashing over the boat covered his words so that no-one heard what it was he said.

Then suddenly everything changed. The turmoil and turbulence abated. The two little boats floated steadily in the water and the furious wind dropped from a whirling frenzy to a fair breeze that would carry them in just the direction they wanted to go.

The monks sat back, soaked and exhausted after all their activity, content to let the sails carry the boats forward with speed and safety.

Comgall called out from the other boat,

'Thank you, Colmcille.'

'Don't thank me, thank the Good Lord.'

Garbhan was shaking his head in disbelief.

'How did you do it, Colmcille? Several times I have travelled this piece of water and each time there have been peculiar winds and currents. How did you manage to control them?'

'Not me! The Good Lord.' said Colmcille repeated

simply and lay down to sleep again.

'Well I'll be blowed,' said Garbhan.

The rest of their journey was uneventful. Wind and current carried them forward as the water narrowed and the trees closed in on them on either side again.

'Will we have more walking to do?' asked Colman, not relishing the prospect.

Garbhan heard the question and said,

'No. This river opens out into Loch Ness. But it is getting dark now and we shall stop soon. I know of a little village by the loch side where we may find shelter and hospitality for the night.'

The village consisted of a few huts gathered together inside a wooden fence to protect the inhabitants from wild animals and perhaps any evil person who might chance that way. As Colmcille's party approached, they were welcomed by a small crowd of villagers who came out to see them.

They seemed friendly but it was once more in Garbhan's hands to translate.

'Tell them we come in peace and in the name of the One True God,' said Colmcille.

'They have heard a little of this God,' said Garbhan after some conversation with their spokesman, 'but they worship their own gods here and have found them to look after them well enough.'

'Let them give us hospitality and in return we shall tell them of the God who is more powerful than all of their gods.'

Garbhan related this to the Pictish leader and he smiled cautiously, nodded, and bade them follow him in.

CHAPTER 9

Danger on the Loch

The hut was dark and smoky inside, lit only by the light from the doorway and the fire that burned in the middle of the floor. They all sank gratefully to the rush-strewn ground round the fire, welcoming the heat of the flames on their sodden clothing. There were several other people, many of them children, in the shadows of the hut, and Colman could see their curious eyes watching the travellers in the firelight.

As the monks looked around them, Garbhan talked slowly and earnestly with the man who had first greeted them. After a while he turned to Colmcille.

'Our host's name is Dorcan and he is pleased to see us. In fact, he is surprised to see us, for he says that there are so many wild things along the way we have come, that he is amazed we have survived, unarmed as we are.'

'Tell him the God who goes with us is mightier than the sword. Ask him too, for that matter, how he manages to live here with his family in such an unprotected kind of house. Surely he too must be troubled by human marauders even if the wooden fence keeps out most of the four-footed kind.'

Garbhan turned and spoke again to Dorcan. He was a small redheaded man with a long flowing red beard to match. His clothes too followed the theme and were dyed in orangey red, yellow and purple. Colman had never seen so many colours at the one time, except perhaps in the rainbow and also in the special Gospel that Colmcille had illuminated and which Diarmaid had shown him. Dorcan's eyes were bright and friendly and sparkled as he spoke animatedly – using his hands to make up for Garbhan's lack of vocabulary with his hands.

'It seems that he lives within the safe sanctuary of a special well,' said Garbhan. 'He says that the spirit of the well protects them from all comers and it is here that the Druids will stop to stay also when they are passing. He says that even those who might not pay heed to the spirit of the well will not offend the host of the Druids. They are much too powerful.'

Druids! Colman pricked up his ears.

'Ask him if he knows of the Druid Broichan!' he interrupted.

When Dorcan heard the name Broichan spoken he turned to Colman with a gabble of words. His voice rose and rose in pitch and all the time he was glancing round nervously as if at any time Broichan himself might appear. Colman cowered, wishing he had not spoken and at the same time fearful for Deirdre in the hands of a man who seemed to put terror into others where ever he went.

When Dorcan had finished Garbhan translated, though he hardly needed to.

'Well Colman you probably got the gist of that.

Broichan is the Chief Druid and the adviser to King Brude. That much we knew already. Our friend here says that he passed this way only recently. He'd been on a raid somewhere and was boasting and showing off a new slave girl he had captured…'

'Deirdre!' gasped Colman. 'Did she have long black hair?'

Garbhan consulted with Dorcan. Colman saw him nod.

'Yes,' replied Garbhan to Colman. 'and she was not being well treated. They were ordering her around. Do this! Get that! Go there! Fetch this! but of course she was foreign and did not understand and then they would push and beat her if she did not do the right thing… which was really all the time.'

Dorcan interrupted and said something more.

'Dorcan says he would have intervened' continued Garbhan ' but Broichan is feared and dreaded. Even now Dorcan is afraid that some of his evil angels may be listening and he dare not say all he would like.'

Dorcan's eyes shifted uneasily around. He muttered something more.

'And now if you don't mind, he would like to change the subject,' said Garbhan.

'Of course, of course,' put in Colmcille who had been listening intently to the exchange of conversation. 'We would not dare to abuse his kind hospitality. But we would like to tell Dorcan that the one true God is mightier than Broichan and his powers of evil. Oh, how I wish I had the language to tell it to him in his own tongue!'

They were given bowls of broth and hard bread to dip in it and as they ate Colmcille explained as well as he could the Gospel message of Christ.

'Unlike the religion of the Druids which is only open to

the select few, the religion of Christ is open to all. Unlike the Druids, the information about our religion is not a secret handed on only by word of mouth, but a formula open to everyone and written down for all to read.'

He reached into his satchel and brought out the gospel that he had been working on. 'Unfortunately it is not yet in your tongue but the day will come when all of your nation will believe in the Christ. How can you do any other when you see that the Christ is more powerful than all your Druids. He is the Arch Druid of all!'

Colman listened only halfheartedly. All the while he saw before him Deirdre tired and beaten in this very house. He looked around him trying to imagine his sister looking round the very same room but he realised almost straightaway that of course she would have had no time for this. However, it seemed at least that she was still alive.

They curled up where they were round the fire that night. Colman was wedged in between Diarmaid and Haldo. Unlike the night before he was as warm as he could be and slept like a log.

He awoke in the morning to the fact that Haldo had gone. He got up quietly without waking the others and went to see if he could find him. He tiptoed carefully out. It was a chilly morning and windy. He pulled his tunic around him tightly and drew up the hood around his ears.

He looked this way and that, but there was no sign of Haldo – no sign of anyone in fact, but he noticed that the door leading out of the enclosure was open and so he went out. Perhaps he had wandered off.

Outside the gate there was still no sign of Haldo but Colman noticed water pouring out of the rock into a stone basin. This must be the well that Dorcan was speaking of last night. He was thirsty, so he decided to have a drink. He was just stooping to scoop some of the clear bubbling water into his hands when a voice said commandingly,

'Wait!'

He jumped. He thought he had been alone. It was Colmcille standing beneath a tree.

'Don't drink yet, my son,' he said. 'Goodness knows what devilish powers that Broichan has bestowed on this well. Let me bless it first.'

He lifted a hand and made the sign of the cross in the air above it, saying a quick prayer of blessing. Then he took a drink from it himself. Colman was about to follow suit when there was a terrible scream from the forest behind the tree where Colmcille had been standing. They looked round, quickly recognising that it was Haldo screaming! Then they heard a crashing noise rapidly approaching them. Colman took a step towards Colmcille, instinct telling him that that would be the safest place to be.

Suddenly Haldo came blundering out, headlong into the clearing where they were standing and fell senseless at Colmcille's feet. From his head there was a stream of blood and there was blood on his sleeve too.

Colman had only time to gasp before a large wild boar came lunging out of the undergrowth after Haldo. It charged for the prone body on the ground and then it stopped in its tracks when it saw Colmcille standing staring at it solidly. It stood transfixed, motionless like a stone, mesmerised by the glare from Colmcille. The abbot raised a hand.

'In the name of the Christ, I charge that whatever evil is in this animal shall be no more.'

Almost immediately the boar – with a mighty roar – slumped to the ground beside Haldo. Colman, horrified, rushed forward to see if the Pictish youth was still alive,

keeping one eye on the boar just in case it should jump up again.

Haldo was completely still. Colmcille came and crouched beside him too.

'Help me to turn him over gently'

As they turned him Haldo moaned and his eyes that had been shut began to flicker.

Colman felt a wave of relief spread over him and he began to shiver with shock. Colmcille meanwhile was undoing the little bag he always carried over his shoulder. Out of it he carefully took a cloth and unwrapped some dried-up looking leaves and flowers.

'What's that?' asked Colman.

The abbot held the little package reverently in his hand. 'This is the herb blessed by St John the Baptist himself. Its healing properties are truly remarkable. I always carry some with me, for you just never know when it might come in handy.'

As he listened to Colmcille, Colman sensed his voice grow strange and faraway sounding. He was also vaguely aware that Diarmaid was bending over Haldo beside him and through a mist he heard Colmcille say,

'Diarmaid, fetch some of that well water quickly!'

The well water was mixed with the herb and a poultice made for Haldo's head and arm.

Colman's head was beginning to spin.

'You'd better get a drink of water for your little friend too,' he said next, and before Colman knew it Diarmaid was bending over him with a cup full of cool clear water. It revived him instantly. He sat up. Haldo too was looking almost as normal and the blood from his head wound had already dried up. He was smiling beneath his bandaged head and gabbled away at them though of course they could not understand a word of what he said.

Soon everyone had recovered enough to continue on their way. The boats were launched and they took their leave of Dorcan who was well pleased with the gift of the large boar with which they had presented him.

It was a stormy day and as they would be sailing on the great Loch Ness Garbhan had informed them that the whole day would be spent in the boat. That in itself was good news. It would be safer, quicker and less tiring than the forest but it was a big loch and could be a rough sail. Not to worry, thought Colman. He was learning like Diarmaid to trust in Colmcille to keep them safe. So while the boat tossed and turned he sat in the bottom with Haldo, exchanging words for 'arm' and 'leg'.

They did indeed make steady going of it and by about midday Colmcille suggested that they put to shore for a rest and some food. They drew the boats up on the pebbly beach.

'Pull them right up,' said Colmcille, 'in case they get caught in the wild waves of this stormy place.' They then sat for a while in the shelter of some bushes and in the lee of a rock. Dorcan's wife had given them a bag of bread that she had baked on a hot stone at the fire in the morning and they ate hungrily. Suddenly Diarmaid nudged Colman.

'Look!' he whispered, pointing out into the loch.

Colman gasped in horror. A large boat was heading in their direction and it seemed to be loaded with well-armed men wearing brightly coloured clothes. Spears bristled from it so that it looked like some large floating hedgehog. Were they men sent from Broichan to find and destroy them?

Colmcille had seen them now too. In an instant he realised the dire situation that they were in. It would give Broichan no better delight than to destroy them all and to

120

produce their heads to King Brude. If Broichan could capture the heads – and therefore the souls which he imagined to be contained in them – of the followers of the White Christ, what power it would give the Druids over the new religion.

'We must crouch down out of sight in these rocks and bushes and then I want you all to sing a hymn with me,' said Colmcille. The monks all looked at him. Was he mad? Was that not the very way to signal just exactly where they were? But Colmcille had started singing and they crouched down, reluctantly and quietly joining in with him.

As they sang Colman could hear the noise of the oars being raised and he imagined that the lookout at the front of the boat would be scanning the very part of the lochside where they were. Thank goodness they had taken the boats right up to the top of the beach.

The boatload of warriors was right beside them now and they could hear what sounded like their leader barking out orders. Colman felt Haldo beginning to get agitated beside him. He must not stand up now and give them all away. He pointed to Haldo's bandaged head and arm and then out to the waters of the loch and hoped that he would understand that there was danger there. He seemed to do so and relaxed again.

They continued singing softly. Colman was surprised that the boatload had not yet heard them. If they could hear the warriors on the boat speaking, surely the people on the boat could hear them sing! The man in charge said something further and there was the noise of oars splashing into the water and the boat rowed steadily away. Colman peeped out. They were leaving!

'Thanks be to the God of all gods!' said Colmcille. 'Right, we can stop singing now.'

'But what happened?' asked Diarmaid. 'Why did they go away? Why didn't they hear us? I don't understand.'

Colman was equally confused. Colmcille was smiling.

'What little faith you boys have.'

'Well I don't understand either,' said Garbhan,' and I heard what the warriors on the boat were saying.'

'Well, what was it?' clamoured Colman and Diarmaid together.

'Well they were indeed from Broichan. Word has gone before us that we are on our way to Brude and that boat had instructions to find us at all costs to prevent us reaching King Brude's court…'

'So why didn't they come ashore?' asked Diarmaid.

'Well that was the peculiar thing. They seemed to think that our singing was a herd of deer calling to each other and the leader shouted out to his men that if there was a herd of deer here there was no possibility of men being here too. Deer are too frightened of men.'

'It is certainly a miracle even though it doesn't say much for our singing,' put in Comgall. 'We thank you, Colmcille.'

'Don't thank me, thank the good Lord. And now Broichan's men with their fancy boat will be well away. Let us make haste to the far shore of the loch for there is a man there who is close to death and I have instructions to go quickly to him and convert him to the new faith before he dies. There is not a moment to lose.'

The monks pushed the boats quickly out into the water and, despite the storm, a gentle wind carried their boats swiftly and smoothly to the far side of the loch. They jumped out. There was a good high piece of open ground from where they could see the land and the loch on all sides.

'We shall camp here for the night,' said Colmcille, 'but have first to go and see the man called Emchad of whom

I have been told. Comgall and Cainnech, you make camp here and look after the others till I return. I don't have to go far from here. Diarmaid, I want you to come with me and Colman and Haldo may come with you too, and of course Garbhan, I need you to translate for me.'

He turned and strode off into the gathering gloom. Diarmaid followed immediately out of habit, and Colman and Haldo trotted behind him. It was Garbhan who hesitated, surprised at this sudden turn of events, just as he was looking forward to some food and a good night's sleep after all the exertion of the day.

'Come! Quickly, Garbhan!' shouted Colmcille from somewhere in the gloom. It was the voice of authority and brooked no arguing. He shrugged his shoulders and taking a last look at the band of monks busy setting up camp for the night he raised a hand in mock farewell to them and set off in the direction of the voice. He was somewhat irritated. He was their guide, not a monk under Colmcille's command. Let the abbot boss the others around. They had chosen to follow him. But let him also remember that Garbhan was still his own man and would not jump at Colmcille's every whim.

He walked slowly. No-one was going to rush him. He met Colmcille and the boys round the first rock that he came to.

'Come on Garbhan!' said Colmcille urgently, and then as if he could read his mind he added, 'I don't ask that you hurry on my account but for the sake of a man called Emchad who lives nearby and is very close to death. Angels are waiting for us at this very minute to come and baptise him so that they might take his soul with them to heaven when he dies. For although he does not know about the One True God, he has led a blameless life and deserves to go to heaven. So, if you will, for his sake, not

123

mine, please hurry. Angels won't wait for ever!'

Ashamed of himself, Garbhan apologised for his slowness and told Colmcille to lead on, he would follow as quickly as he could.

Colmcille took him at his word and despite being in a strange country set off at a determined pace. Garbhan strode out behind him with Diarmaid and Haldo at his heels. Colman, the smallest, had to trot to keep up, scared that if he fell behind in the darkness he might never see any of them again.

It seemed a long while struggling through damp and scratchy undergrowth until they reached a little hut in a clearing at the top of a steep slope.

'This is the place,' said Colmcille, as he bent to enter the hut.

Inside all was quiet and Colman realised then that there had been a loud wind outside in the trees, noticeable now by its absence.

Colmcille went straight over to a pile of heather at one side of the smoke filled room where an old thin man was lying. Beside him stood two women who were both weeping, and at his feet a solemn younger man with a concerned expression on his face.

They looked up, surprised, at the entry of the strangers but there was no hostility in their grief stricken faces.

'The Peace of the Lord be upon this house and all who are in it,' said Colmcille briefly. 'We have been called to come to Emchad.' Garbhan translated quickly.

The man at the end of the bed looked towards them curiously.

'But he is dying!' Garbhan repeated the speech to Colmcille.

'I know. That's why we are here. Angels are waiting to take the soul of your father to heaven where he will live for ever but they cannot do that until he is baptised...'

'But how do you know that he is my father...' exclaimed the man looking round at Garbhan for some kind of support. Garbhan pulled a face and shrugged. He was certain he didn't know but he had seen enough of the workings of Colmcille by now to reserve judgement on every strange happening.

'We shall talk in a minute about that,' said Colmcille to the man. 'We have no time to waste just now. Quickly, Garbhan! Translate as fast as you can.' With concerned expression Colmcille beckoned Garbhan down to the level of the poor man in the bed.

'Emchad, can you hear me?' said Colmcille. Garbhan spoke. The man nodded. 'We come to bring you good news. News of a God who is goodness itself and who has overcome the darkness of death. Can you believe in such a God?'

After hearing the question, Emchad began muttering. Garbhan bent over him. 'He says that he always suspected there was something more. He believes you.'

'Good,' said Colmcille and he crouched down over the bed and taking a phial of water out of the folds of his cloak he poured it over the head of the man in the bed.

'In the name of the Father, the Son and the holy Ghost! I baptise you, Emchad. May your soul arrive in peace at its heavenly home!'

Emchad opened his eyes widely and looked up into the face of Colmcille. Then he gazed slowly round the room smiling at the women who had stopped sobbing now in their surprise and at the man at the foot of his bed. A strange light began to fill the room. Emchad was looking up now above them all and his face was radiant. Colman, Diarmaid and Haldo turned to see what he was looking at but there was nothing. The light faded and they looked back at Emchad. His eyes were closed now and there was a smile on his face.

'May the God of all beginnings and of all ends be with you on your last long journey, Emchad!' whispered Colmcille then he bowed his head. For a moment the room was filled with silence. Then Colman was once more aware of the wind blowing faintly outside in the trees.

'He is gone!' Colmcille stood up, almost it seemed, in relief that the thing that he had been called to do had successfully been done.

The two women at the bedside burst out into sobs again. The man who had been standing took a step towards Colmcille, a strange look on his face. For a moment Colman thought he was going to accuse Colmcille of killing the man in the bed, perhaps even hit him, but instead he said,

'Baptise me too Stranger' pointing to his forehead. Colmcille did not need a translation. His meaning was clear enough.

Colmcille looked taken aback now and spoke to Garbhan. 'But doesn't he want to hear what it is all about?'

The man shook his head and spoke slowly and deliberately to Garbhan.

'He says that he never saw such a look of happiness on his father's face as he had at the end, so it must be a happy place to go. If his father has gone there, he wants to ensure that when his time comes, he and his whole family will be in the same place with him.'

Colmcille smiled, 'Well I have heard of many reasons but never this. This man has faith without having even heard the Gospel of Christ. Tell him I shall baptise him and his family, and one day I shall send a missionary who can speak his language to preach to him and his people. A curse on me that I cannot speak to him as easily as I would like. What is his name?'

Garbhan consulted with the man.

'It is Fearalac.'

Colmcille took out the phial he had with him once more and baptised Fearalac and his family in turn, including all the small children. Then they took their leave of the household, promising to send a missionary to that part of the country as soon as it could be arranged.

The night was very dark now and the wind was howling in the trees. As they left the warmth and safety of the little house Colman wondered if they would ever find their way back to the camp site.

CHAPTER 10

The Water Horse

Colman need not have worried. Fearalac insisted on travelling with them to show them the way. It seemed a much longer journey back and Colman wondered all the way at what he had seen. Strange things were happening and Colmcille had an uncanny way of knowing just how things would turn out.

Fearalac showed them back to the loch side and then melted away into the blackness after thanking Colmcille yet again. They found the others mostly asleep in the shelter of a big rock. Cainnech was awake keeping watch for them and he seemed pleased to see them.

'Thank goodness you're back safely,' he said 'I had a terrible worry that some wild animal might get you… or worse, Morrigan… and then what would we have done?'

Colmcille patted him on the shoulder.

'Cainnech, I am surprised at you. I have just baptised a heathen man who was trusting God to take him all the way

128

to heaven and you cannot even trust Him to take us a few miles. Shame on you! Now you go to sleep! I go to pray alone.'

His tone of voice left no room for argument and they watched him turn down to the water's edge which sparkled in the weak moonlight.

Colman found it hard to sleep that night and yet he must have dozed off for he was woken in the morning by Haldo who was shaking him none too gently.

The weather was still as wild as it had been the night before and Colman was intrigued to see what Colmcille would do about it for he was sure that he would be able to change the weather to suit them. But nothing happened.

'Put out to sea!' commanded Colmcille and the monks, surprised at the command, looked from one to the other. Surely he didn't mean them to go out in this storm? It was suicide.

Colmcille guessed what they were thinking and added sharply,

'The Lord wishes us to go on this journey and if this is the weather he wishes us to travel in, then travel we shall. So let us get started immediately or we shall get nowhere today.'

Against all the odds they managed to get the boats out on to the tossing waves. The wind was too strong for the sails so they rowed halfheartedly, finding that for all the rowing that they did, they stayed in exactly the same spot.

'This is hopeless,' said Garbhan after a while, expressing the views of them all. Colmcille stood at the front of their boat and pretended not to hear. Perhaps he could not hear above the noise of the wind and the waves. The monks continued rowing despondently, their spirits sinking with each stroke. They even had to begin to bale as water came splashing in over the sides. If Colmcille would not or could not save them, who would?

Suddenly Colman saw a black shape in the water. It was far off but approaching rapidly. Was it a monster?

He staggered up the heaving boat to the prow and pointed it out to Colmcille. The latter did not seem unduly surprised or alarmed.

As the shape drew nearer they could see that it was a horse. Colman gasped. So, at last! One of the great Water Horses that he had heard about in stories. There was magic in them, people said, so he stepped behind Colmcille and peered out warily at the approaching beast.

It was a large black stallion. It drew alongside them and then spoke, snorting all the time,

'It is spread around the country that the great Colmcille is journeying this way and I came to see the holy man. Is he here?'

'I am he,' replied Colmcille, 'and please tell me why you are staring at us?'

I came to offer you my service. Your fame goes before you, holy Colmcille, but... excuse my asking... what are you trying to do here, turning round and round with your boats in the water? I saw you with my extended sight from the other end of the loch and in the time it has taken me to swim up to you, you have travelled nowhere and done nothing. I don't understand!'

The monks were taken aback. Was it not painfully obvious what they were trying to do? It was Garbhan who spoke with the exasperation that they all felt.

'Wild beast, whoever you are, you are the first one today to have said something sensible. You are quite right. We are puddling around here getting wet and cold and, if anything, further from our destination than we were this morning.' He glowered in Colmcille's direction.

Colmcille spoke, 'What Garbhan is trying to say is that

these are our boats and that we are attempting to reach the far end of this loch but that the wind and waves are against us and that we lack your power to move as we would wish.'

The Water Horse snorted. 'Is that all? I shall be glad to help then. Perhaps I could tow you.'

'I've seen it all now,' said Garbhan to himself. 'A speaking horse who is offering to tow us!' But his cynicism quickly changed to astonishment when he saw the Water Horse vanish before his eyes and its place taken by a muscular-looking man who rose and sank effortlessly on the waves.

'Who is this now?' he wondered, and then the youth spoke and he knew from the same whinnying tone that this man was the horse in a different form.

'I have to change form to get hands for tying,' explained the man, 'Give me your mooring ropes.' Colmcille and Comgall leant out and handed the man the ropes and he tied them both on to a stout stick which just happened to be floating past in the water; nobody was surprised at the coincidence. Having done that deftly, with a terrible splash he transformed back into the Water Horse. With a final neigh he shouted above the storm,

'Hold on!' and taking the stick between his teeth he set off up the loch. It was all the monks could do to hold on as their boats tossed and bumped over the waves. Soon they seemed to be going so fast that they were gliding over the top of the water, hardly touching the waves at all. Then it became so smooth that they could sit up with ease and look around them.

On either side of the loch the high forested slopes of the mountains sped by and Colman's first thought was that this would certainly get rid of Morrigan. It was a couple of days since they had seen her but there was every chance that she would be following them still.

In no time at all they reached the end of the loch and the stallion drew them up safely on to the beach. He shook himself and gave a whinny.

'There you are now. If someone could just untie me that would save me going to the trouble of changing form again.'

It was Haldo the Horseman who stepped forward automatically, his eyes shining. He patted the noble beast who glistened with wetness and slowly untied the boats from his makeshift harness.

'I thank you, kind sir,' said the Water Horse stepping back. 'I can see you are good with horses but sense that horses have not always been good to you. Who knows how things may turn out?' He turned to Colmcille

'I am glad to have been able to help you, holy Colmcille. Perhaps if you pass this way again we shall meet another time. And now I must be off.' He began to paw the ground with his hoof. Colmcille raised a hand in blessing. 'The blessing of God on you, noble Water Horse. We thank you for your help. Go forth in peace.'

The Water Horse bowed its head, its long flowing mane blowing out in the wind. 'Farewell!' he cried into the wind, then turned and in the twinkling of an eye was lost to view in the stormy waters of the loch.

For a while the monks stared after him in stunned silence. Then Diarmaid whistled between his teeth,

'Whew! Did you ever see the like of that!!'

They all broke out into excited conversation save for Haldo who stood still, staring at the place where the beast had entered the water.

'Right,' said Colmcille above their babbling ' Thanks to our friend, we are here a lot sooner than we expected How far do we have to go, Garbhan?'

'Not far. In fact, the boats should be able to navigate the river till we come quite close to the fort of King Brude. If we're lucky we should reach it before nightfall. If we meet any more of your friends, Colmcille, we may even be there sooner.'

Colmcille laughed at the expression on his face. 'Come on let's get moving.'

In good spirits they launched the boats again and steered them to the river that led from the end of the loch. It was easy going and once in the river they sped along in the current, merely using the oars to steer away from rocky parts. Here in the river, and sheltered by forest and hill on both sides, the day did not seem nearly so stormy and rough as it had been on the loch.

The air was warmer and they relaxed a little but they were now very much in King Brude's territory and anything could happen. Just occasionally out of the corner of his eye, Colman thought he saw a movement in the bushes beside the river but when he looked straight at it there was nothing. As they continued however, the uneasy feeling grew. It was with a jolt of horror that he saw the large black bird sitting ahead of them on a dead branch overhanging the river.

Colman tapped Diarmaid on the shoulder and pointed the bird out.

'Is it Her?' he asked in a whisper.

Diarmaid with a serious look on his face nodded. 'I think so,' he whispered, 'Better tell Colmcille!'

One glance showed that Colmcille had already seen. He signalled to them to pull the boats into the bank. Then he spoke to them.

'As you see, my brothers, Morrigan still hovers hopefully round our party. I somehow thought she would not give up that easily. We shall have to sail past her now but we shall go as before, singing psalms, and the Lord will protect us. Be of good courage!'

They set off at first hesitantly and Colman's heart sank when he saw that the river in front of the place where Morrigan sat was white with turbulent water. Did she know that some accident was about to happen? Could she make it happen?

Above his worried thoughts and the noise of the splashing river, he was aware of a faint singing. It was growing in strength. Then he realised it was coming from the other monks, but how softly! It would need to be louder than that to thwart Morrigan! He broke into a lusty tune. He would show her! He was no longer aware of the roughness of the water; he did not even notice when they had passed Morrigan. He shut his eyes, daring not to look. Suddenly he felt the boat pull to a halt as it hit the bank.

'We're past her!' It was Diarmaid. A loud cheer went up from them all. Colmcille came over to Colman

'Well my Little Colm,' he said, 'That was some singing you were doing! Did you see how Morrigan shrank from us as we went past? I'll be bound that it was mostly your doing.' Colman blushed at the compliment, and also with shame because he had not been brave enough to look Morrigan in the face.

They set off again, every one of them now confident that they would overcome anything. They rounded a bend in the river and Garbhan pointed out a hill top to them all. On it they could see buildings and a trail of smoke rising into the air.

'That's it!' he cried. 'The Great Fortress of King Brude, High King of the Picts!'

They all stared at it in awe. Here was the end of their journey at last. What were they going to find? Colman of course, could only think of one thing and that was

Deirdre. Was she going to be here? He dared not hope when so soon that hope might be dashed.

'It's too late in the day to approach the fort now,' said Colmcille looking up at the sky which was beginning to cloud over for the night. 'By the time we landed the boats and walked up to it, it would be completely dark. Is there anywhere we can rest safely for the night, Garbhan? You've been here before.'

Garbhan looked around quickly. 'As it so happens, there are some little islands over here if we steer this way.' He pointed over to their right. 'We will be safe there from wild animals, I should think.'

With a bit of deft oarsmanship they managed to steer their boats through the fast flowing river towards one of the islands.

It seemed strange to be on dry land again for they had spent practically the whole of the last two days on the water, and as usual, Colman still felt the rocking of the boat in his body long after he had actually left it.

He felt exhausted and he was hungry as well. 'Thank goodness we've stopped,' he said, 'I don't think I could have faced a long trek into the fort. I'm so hungry!'

'Well don't set your hopes too high,' retorted Diarmaid, 'We've no food left.'

Colman groaned and clutched his stomach which was by now beginning to ache. Just then Haldo came rushing up to them. He was leaping about excitedly,

'What is it, Haldo?' said Colman, puzzled by his behaviour. Haldo was gabbling away in Pictish.

'What's he trying to say?' shouted Diarmaid to Garbhan.

'Come over and see for yourselves,' answered Garbhan grinning. The two boys went over to join the rest of their party. They were crowded round something on th

136

ground. They made room for Haldo as he pulled his intrigued friends towards them. There, lying shiny in the dusk, was a large salmon, perhaps the largest that Colman had ever seen. He gasped, impressed.

'How did you catch that?' he asked.

'It was Haldo,' chorused some of the others. 'It just seemed to jump out of the river almost straight into his arms.' It seemed a fitting omen for the last night of their journey.

Colman went to bed full and satisfied. Tomorrow perhaps... Deirdre...? But even the excitement of that possibility was not enough to ward off the sleep of exhaustion that overtook him as soon as he lay down on the pile of leaves and branches that they had gathered together for bedding.

He was first awake in the morning. He sat up and looked around. Even Colmcille was still asleep on the ground beside them. How could he sleep so soundly when there might be wild beasts or even Morrigan abroad to pounce on them all unwary? Up till now Colmcille had watched over them each night on the trip and they had felt safe, knowing that he was in charge. Now Colman realised that no-one had thought to ask if he were tired too or if some of them might not take his place as night watch.

Colmcille woke and sat up. Colman said to him,

'If you had told me, Colmcille, that you were tired and wanted to rest, I should gladly have taken your place on the night watch.'

Colmcille laughed, a merry laugh in the crisp morning air. It seemed to mingle with the rippling of the river as it passed by their island resting place.

'You, my Little Colm, would not have been fit to guard a fly last night. Why, you went to sleep with a piece of salmon half eaten in your hand! Besides, I knew that these islands would be peaceful and shelter us safely.'

He stood up and raised a hand.

'May the Lord bless these islands which have protected us this night from all onslaughts of the devil. May they remain for ever green and forever a haven of rest so that even though the waters of the river may rise in turbulent times and swamp them they will always return again to their peaceful green and be even more beautiful each time.'

Colmcille lowered his hand and wandered quietly away. Colman made to say something more to him but a hand on his shoulder made him turn. It was Comgall.

'Leave him be just now,' said the older man. 'He has slept all night and now he needs time to himself to think and to pray. Today is going to be a big day for him and it is important to him that he prepares well for it.' He hesitated for a moment before continuing, 'Today is going to be a big day for you too, I think, isn't it?'

Colman nodded glumly. He wasn't sure how he was going to cope with today. Perhaps he needed to go apart like Colmcille and prepare too…'

Comgall was watching him and smiled.

'Don't worry Colman. All will work out in the Lord's good time. You'll see.'

Colman wandered off to find Diarmaid and Haldo. He found them at the water's edge throwing little pebbles into the river. They seemed pensive too. What was happening to them all? Were they all going to have last minute nerves? Now, if ever, Colmcille needed them. It was with a forced joviality that Colman addressed them,

'So here you two are! All set for the big day?'

Haldo grinned at him and he smiled back. Diarmaid scowled.

'Will you stop being so cheerful Colman! Do you realis

138

that this may be our last day of freedom, our last day of life in fact. We are about to approach and enter the fort of the most powerful King of Pictland and here we are, a band of weary travellers, unprotected and unarmed. If they don't like the look of us, it's the end of everything for us all.' He drew a little stick absentmindedly through the water as he crouched at the river edge. Colman was surprised. It was not like Diarmaid to be so downcast.

'Oh come on, Diarmaid! Isn't it you who always says Colmcille can do this and Colmcille can do that? Even I who have only known him for a few days have seen him order the wind about, kill wild animals with a single stare, even predict the future. Don't tell me he doesn't know what he's doing. We'll be all right, you'll see.' He wished he was as confident as he sounded but Diarmaid jumped up lightly, almost as if a weight was off his shoulders.

'You're right of course, Colman. And I am a stupid idiot not to trust in Colmcille's judgement.'

It was a while before Colmcille was ready to leave and as they waited for him, they sat watching the fort to which they would soon be climbing. It was not the only fort that they could see by any manner of means. There were several hills in their sight and each had a fortification on it.

'King Brude governs them all,' explained Garbhan, 'and with them can control this part of the country for he has a lookout on every hilltop. The one there to which we are going,' he pointed, 'is the largest and the one he stays in most of the time when he is not touring his territories... or fighting the Scots of Dalriada!'

It looked large and forbidding. Was Deirdre there, Colman wondered? And if she was, how was she faring? Dorcan at Loch Ness had said she was being kicked and beaten. Would she still be alive? Would she be the same person that he knew and loved, or would she have lost her senses just as Haldo had done after being kicked by a horse? It didn't bear thinking about.

When Colmcille was at length ready, they launched the boats once more. The swiftness of the current was going to carry them down river away past the fort so that they would have to double back by land and, what was worse, would have to carry their boats with them. They could not risk leaving them unguarded for who knew how many days and nights they would be in the fort.

So it was that late afternoon found them toiling up the hill towards the fort.

They followed a well-trodden track and Garbhan said that this would lead them right to the gates of the fort. It seemed a bit strange that they had seen nobody nor been challenged by any guard. After a while it began to feel downright uncanny. There was the feeling of something hanging in the air about to happen.

'I don't like this,' whispered Colman to Diarmaid as they panted up the steep path. Then gradually they were aware of an eerie kind of singing coming to them on the air over the walls of the fort, although there was no-one to be seen.

'Druids!' whispered Diarmaid in awe to Colman.

Colmcille had heard it too, and suggested that since it was about time for evening prayers, they sing a psalm.

'Something appropriate!' he added with a twinkle in his eye.

He led them off in the singing,

'Beautiful words fill my mind as I compose this
song for the king,
Like the pen of a good writer my tongue is ready
with a poem.'

The others joined in, gaining courage as they went:

'Buckle on your sword, mighty king; you are
    glorious and majestic…
… Your arrows are sharp, they pierce the hearts of
    your enemies; nations fall down at your feet…'

Soon they discovered that the louder they sang, the
louder came the singing from inside the fort. They
increased the volume,

'You, my king, will have many sons to succeed your
    ancestors as kings, and you will make them rulers
    over the whole earth.'

So that was how it was going to be. They did not have
swords so they would have a battle of voices instead.
Colman noticed Colmcille's voice was now thundering
out, so much so that the rest of them were completely
swamped by it, never mind the Druids within.

'My song will keep your fame alive for ever, and
    every one will praise you for all time to come.'

They rounded off the psalm in full voice just as they
approached the main gates of the fortress and their spirits
were very much lighter. God was indeed with them – they
could feel it. The thick wooden gates were firmly barred
and bolted but they did not worry. After all, Colmcille
would soon deal with them.

Colmcille stepped forward ahead of the band and
struck the doors with his staff. Nothing happened.

'I can still hear singing from inside,' said Colman as
they waited.

'Huh! Druids! Call that singing?' cried Colmcille, anger
beginning to rise in him now. He had expected perhaps
a hostile reception. He had not expected no reception at
all.

'Discourtesy was not one of the attributes of the hon-
ourable King Brude whose fame I heard about.' he
shouted in a voice filled with ire. Still nothing happened.

The doors remained tightly bolted although the singing had stopped.

Colmcille's face darkened. Was he going to curse the King? Quickly Colman tapped him on the sleeve.

'Colmcille,' he said timidly, fearful in case the holy man's wrath might be turned on him, 'they won't understand you. Get Garbhan to translate.'

Colmcille turned, surprised to see Colman there. In his anger he had forgotten all about his companions. He softened a little,

'You're right, but I'm sure they must have got the gist of that. After all, King Brude would have interpreters of his own, you would think. However, Garbhan, give it a go.'

Garbhan shouted something out. His voice was weak compared to Colmcille's but it was loud enough to carry over the walls.

Still no action.

'Right,' said Colmcille striding forward to the gates. His face was grim, although he had lost the rage of impetuousness. Boldly he traced the sign of the cross on the doors and then knocking again with his staff, he laid his hand upon it.

There was a deep rumbling which seemed to shake the very ground on which they were standing. Diarmaid and Colman clutched Haldo who stood between them grinning. Suddenly to their amazement they could hear the sound of heavy bolts being drawn back. Aha! so the Picts had relented after all!

The doors swung slowly open. Astonished, the little band of monks looked into the first enclosure of the fort and saw guards running for their lives away from them, turning every so often with panic-stricken faces towards their visitors.

142

Colman gaped. So, the guards didn't open the doors! Then who did?'

There was no time to wonder. Colmcille strode purposefully through the entrance.

'Come on brothers, follow me!'

CHAPTER 11

At the Court of King Brude

Colman and Diarmaid kept closely behind Colmcille as he marched into the fort. His anger seemed to have faded now and they sensed he was feeling like a victor. On all sides they were conscious of being watched although they saw no-one apart from the fleeing guards.

There were stone walls and huts all around them as they continued up the hill and entered a second enclosure which was broader and flatter. To one side there was a larger hall and out of it came a little party of very finely dressed men. Leading them was a tall dark man whose clothes were of every colour of the rainbow. Colman noticed that round his neck he wore a heavy chain of lustrous metal. On both his arms he had shiny armlets and they glinted in the fading light as the last rays of the setting sun disappeared under the horizon. Was this the King?

Colmcille halted and waited for the group to come to him. Colman was aware of the abbot pulling himself up to his full height. What was going to happen?

'Is this the discourteous way in which the King of all Pictland treats a visiting personage of the royal line of Niall of the Nine Hostages?' asked Colmcille imperiously. Garbhan was at his side translating as quickly as he could but Colmcille had launched into a further speech before he could get it all out.

'Hospitality,' he continued, 'the mark of a truly great king, seems to be singularly lacking here!'

The man with the rainbow-coloured cloak at the head of the little Pictish party looked a bit sheepish and apologetic. He gabbled something.

Garbhan told them that the man was the spokesman for King Brude and the lack of welcome had been on the advice of the great Arch Druid Broichan who had suggested bolting the doors against Colmcille and his party as a test of his magic.

'Huh!' sneered Colmcille savouring the moment, 'and I hope the King now sees whose 'magic' as you call it is the stronger.'

'Indeed,' said the man, 'he is having words with Broïchan at this very moment, and in recompense for not having opened the gates to you, he requests that you come and tell him about your god after you have refreshed yourselves from your journey.'

Colman saw that Colmcille was satisfied. And no wonder! He had just pulled off a spectacular stunt which had showed him to be more powerful than the Druid Broichan. His royal blood already gave him a status equal to Brude himself. Now he had his audience with the King which was the reason that they had come; and gave him a good vantage point from which to claim the isle of Iona for his monastic settlement.

They were shown the well where they could drink and,

after they had been there for a while, the Pict with the fine clothes who had spoken to them before came to them and said something more.

'We are requested to join the King now ' said Garbhan.

They followed the man over the sloping yard to the large hall from which the party of men had previously emerged.

As they were approaching it, another couple of men came out, one small and one very large. They were backing out of the door. Once they were out they turned and Colman gasped. He could see their faces clearly and the taller man had a deep purple mark over half of his face. It was the face he would never forget.

'It's him,' he croaked hoarsely but no-one seemed to hear.

Colmcille was striding out ahead of him and Colman ran forward and caught hold of his sleeve.

'That's he, Colmcille! The man who took Deirdre! Ask if she's here. Tell the King she is my sister.'

Colmcille stopped and turned gently to the boy.

'I will see what can be done, never fear Little Colm. But for now don't do anything to let that evil man suspect that we know about Deirdre. If he holds her in this place he may order his men to take her away so that we can't get her. I shall speak to King Brude himself about her – among other things. Don't worry.' He laid an arm gently on Colman's shoulder. From the touch Colman felt a wave of relief spread through his body. The matter was now in higher hands. It would all be well. He had worried for weeks. Now he could do no more.

All the same, he shuddered at the face of the man as he now glowered at them. Broichan said something to Colmcille and the evil in his voice was apparent as the two men stared at each other. Garbhan started to translate but

Colmcille stopped him. He smiled an over-polite smile at the Druid.

'No thank you, Garbhan. I don't think we want that translated.' He bent to enter the door of the hall and the rest of the monks followed. Colman kept close by the abbot as they looked round in the semi-darkness. There were torches flaring on each side of the room and it seemed even larger than it had looked from the outside.

A deep booming voice shouted something from one end of the room. Seated on a chair sat a large redheaded man with a beard that reached to his waist. The beard was shaking, and they realised that it was he that had spoken. Around his neck was a heavy golden chain and, on his arm, armlets that were bigger and shinier than those worn by the man outside. A group of warriors sat on the floor around him looking curiously at the party that had just entered. All were dressed in the same kind of multi-coloured clothes as the spokesman whom they had already met.

'The great High King Brude of the Pictish Realms welcomes Colmcille, Prince of the line of Niall of the Nine Hostages' translated Garbhan quickly as the King stood up to greet Colmcille.

'And priest of the one true God.' added Colmcille as they clasped arms. It was translated to the King.

'Hmm...' said Brude '... so they say, and I can tell you that no such priest would have come into my stronghold alive were it not for his royal blood. I offer royal courtesy to you as befits one of your rank. As to your God – well, I did have my ideas about that, but having seen the power with which you opened my gates, I am prepared now to listen at least.' He had been speaking affably to them. Suddenly his face fell. He seemed to be peering at something over Colmcille's shoulder. They all turned to follow

147

his gaze. He was looking at Haldo, who stood smirking as usual.

King Brude took a step towards him.

'Haldo?' The boy grinned back but did not seem to recognise him. Brude turned to Colmcille. 'It's Haldo, isn't it? My son! What's wrong with him? He doesn't seem himself. He doesn't even recognise me!' Colmcille explained briefly what Moluag had told them about the kick from a horse that he had received on the head. Brude nodded, concerned. He had seen many such injuries before, especially in battle.

'Will he always be like this?' he asked through the interpreter.

'Maybe yes, maybe no,' was all Colmcille could reply.

'Moluag felt he would be better among his own people,' added Comgall who had been in Lìos Mòr when the accident had happened. Brude nodded again.

'We thank you for bringing him. We will look after him.' He grasped Haldo by the shoulders. For a moment the boy looked into his face and frowned, squinting at his father as if somewhere in his memory something was stirring. It only lasted briefly and then he began making faces once more as he pulled jerkily out of the King's clutch to stand beside Colman and Diarmaid again.

The King sighed, turned to Garbhan, and said something.

'His Royal Highness would like to learn about our Christ without more ado,' said their guide with a note of triumph. 'He says, please, will you all be seated.'

They sat down on the rush-strewn floor and Colmcille began, pausing only to allow Garbhan his interpreter time to catch up with what he had said, and Colman could see that even having to stop for that long made him impatient. The abbot explained how, unlike Druidism, Christianity was for everyone, not just the chosen few, and that was why they took great pains to write out all the sacred writings. The Druids, he said, keep all their learning in their heads so that no-one but they know it.'

He went into his satchel and drew out the book which he had brought specially for the occasion. In it were the psalms carefully copied in his own hand.

'This is a present from me to you, King Brude. These are some of our sacred writings and you can have them.' He began to read the psalm that they had sung on the way up to the fortress and as the interpreter translated, he could see the King was taking a very keen interest indeed.

'One day, if you wish, I shall send you a scribe who can write the psalms for you in your own Pictish tongue.'

'What must I do to follow your Christ?' he asked.

'I will instruct you in His ways and then if you wish to follow Him you must be baptised.'

'So be it,' said the King. 'Instruct me!'

Long and earnestly Colmcille spoke with the King and his baptism was set for the following day. He would show them a suitably clear spring that they could use.

A proclamation was sent out the next morning. All the King's subjects that were in the fort were summoned to be baptised too but Colmcille was adamant that he must preach to them first.

'You cannot order people to believe in Christ,' he told the king. 'They must believe in Him in their own hearts.'

Brude agreed to let Colmcille speak to the people first. Word went around and Colmcille chose a little hill on the far side of the river from the fort for his preaching place. He wanted to be well away from any of the forts so that no-one would feel pressurised by the King to be baptised or hindered by Broichan. There the grass had been grazed down by animals and there was plenty of room for people

149

to sit. Brude had told them that they would find a boat down by the river to use for the crossing and so they set off.

Colman skipped along happily beside Diarmaid. As they went down from the fort, people could already be seen gathering on the hill on the other side of the river. Word had travelled fast and everyone came, curious to see the strangers who had magic that was even more powerful than that of Broichan the Purple.

They were only half-way to the riverbank when suddenly a shout of alarm went up. There were shrieks of terror and panic. The people on the far side could be seen running down to the water's edge and there was quite a bit of commotion on their own side also. When they reached the water's edge they discovered a crowd of people lifting a man on to a bier. The man was covered in blood and all around him there was a wailing of grieving friends and relatives.

Garbhan asked them what had happened, for it was clear that the man was but a youth and there had obviously been an accident of some kind.

'He was swimming across the river,' one man managed to stutter 'and then... and then... the monster of the river rose out of the water,' and he demonstrated the size of the monster with his arms, his eyes wide with fear,' and he was crushed by its powerful jaws, and though we managed to put out in a boat and rescue his body, he was already dead by the time we got him ashore.'

Colmcille's little party gaped in horror. They still had to cross the river themselves. At least, thought Colman we should be safe in a boat. Then they looked up and down and realised that there was no boat. The boat that had brought the dying man had crossed again to the other side with people wanting to hear the preaching of Colmcille.

Colmcille turned to his friends, 'Lugne,' he said,' will you please swim across and fetch the little boat which is moored over yonder at the bank?' Almost with one voice everyone cried out, 'No!'

'Colmcille, are you off your head?' said Comgall, voicing the feelings of them all, 'There is a dangerous monster in those waters. It has already killed one man who was swimming across today. It is not fair on Lugne. We can easily wait until they bring the boat over for us again.'

Colmcille said nothing but gave his elder a stubborn look that the other knew only too well. Comgall was used to going along with Colmcille's sometimes odd ideas, but this was going a bit too far.

Before he had time to protest further there was a splash as Lugne dived into the river, stripped of all his clothes except his short tunic. With their hearts in their mouths and in complete silence, they watched as with strong strokes the youthful swimmer pulled away from the shore. It seemed like an age to the onlookers but in fact it did not take him long to reach the middle of the river, where he seemed to be fighting the current rather than any monster.

Suddenly Colman noticed a large black shape circling above them.

'Morrigan!' he shouted pointing and then repeated, 'Morrigan!' his throat now so dry with alarm that he could only whisper. In that same moment there was a swirling of the waters beside Lugne. It was certainly not the current and in an instant a large head and long neck shot out of the water. All Colman was aware of was a flashing eye and wide gaping jaw with a row of very sharp teeth. He looked in horror as it towered over Lugne's bravely swimming form. Morrigan all the while flew overhead, croaking, it seemed, in glee.

They all froze, waiting for the monster to strike, and

151

were only dimly aware of Colmcille standing up at his full height beside them. The abbot raised his arm in the air and made the sign of the cross in the direction of the fearsome beast,

'I command you to go no further nor will you touch so much as a hair of that man! Go back to where you belong, fearful monster of the deep!'

The monster stopped in its tracks, its flashing eyes dimming with surprise as it turned at the sound of Colmcille's mighty voice. Then, with a frightening splashing of water, it shot off backwards almost as if someone were jerking it back with a rope. Morrigan disappeared into the distance with it, croaking in dismay as she went. By the time the terrible twosome were out of sight, Lugne had reached the other side and had jumped into the boat. As he brought it back to ferry his friends across, he was met by a loud cheering which was echoed on the other side of the river where the waiting crowd had seen everything that had happened.

After that Colmcille found that his lack of the Pictish language hindered him not one bit and the Pictish people, convinced by what they had witnessed, came forward as one, to be baptised. Never before had they seen such wonders and they were convinced by Colmcille's actions more than by any of his words, that here was a power ever more powerful than Broichan's.

There was a distinct air of gaiety that afternoon as the all trooped out of the forts towards the well for baptism. Only Broichan and his household didn't join in. From high on the hillside, he watched, resplendent in his best finery, calling down curses on Colmcille and shouting that Brude would live to regret this.

Despite Broichan the baptism went ahead without hitch and afterwards, in high spirits, everyone wende

their way back towards Brude's fort. Tonight the King was throwing a feast for them all. There would be singing and music and food such as the little party of travellers from Iona had never seen, they were told.

The smell of roast boar met them as they entered the fortress once again and Colman's stomach began to ache with the thought of the feast.

'I don't think I can wait that long,' he said to Diarmaid. Diarmaid agreed.

'To think that we were scared of coming here,' he said, 'I can't think when we've had such a good time. Though if it hadn't been for Colmcille, I suspect our heads might have been swinging over the gateposts by now.'

Colman gulped at the thought.

'No sign of Deirdre either,' he said, mournfully remembering his reason for coming here. Colmcille had been so preoccupied with the baptism that Colman hadn't liked to keep pestering him to find out whether he had asked King Brude about Deirdre.

Tables had been set out for the feast in the King's Hall. Broichan sat on one side of the king with Colmcille on the other. Broichan, glowering, showed his disapproval of the king's actions that afternoon. But Brude was cheerful and seemed to pay no heed to his Advisor.

Colmcille said little, just enough to reassure the king that if he would stand firm in his new beliefs, the Druid would be unable to touch him with his powers.

The meal went well. Colman and Diarmaid, seated near Colmcille, had never seen such an amount of food.

'This really is the hospitality worthy of a High King,' said Diarmaid happily as he munched on a bone and Colman was just in the middle of agreeing when suddenly he jumped up. He shook the table as he rose and his plate went clattering to the floor.

'Deirdre!' he shouted. Diarmaid glanced up at the commotion and saw that his friend was staring at one of the serving maids who stood behind Broichan. The girl looked tired, hollow eyed and sad. Then she saw Colman. The transformation was immediate! Her eyes lit up first in surprise, then in disbelief, and finally, joy. She took a step towards Colman but Broichan had seen what was happening and pulled her back by her hair, saying some sort of command in Pictish. She shrank back, suddenly remembering where she was, and the solemn look came down on her face like a curtain.

Colman rushed over towards his sister, shouting angrily at the Arch Druid as he went. But he did not reach her. Two strong guards of Broichan's household stepped forward and grabbed him by the arms and started to drag him out of the hall.

Colmcille had seen everything and, with Garbhan's help, quickly explained things. It seemed an age before the King cried out 'Halt!' and the guards waited, looking from him towards their own master, wondering what to do. There was then some discussion between the King and Broichan and the outcome was that Colman was allowed to stay while his sister was led out.

Colman was distraught. 'She is my sister!' he wailed. 'That man stole her! Please Colmcille, do something!'

He was led back to his seat and Broichan's guards stood behind him to ensure he did not try to escape.

Colmcille spoke to him. 'I'm afraid the King says it is not in his power to release one of Broichan's household and Broichan says he will certainly not set free his best slave. Never fear, though! She is alive. At least we know that now, and we have still some time here. All is not yet lost!'

Colman was not so sure. For the next few days,

Colmcille and Brude talked together, mainly about the Kingdom of Dalriada. But they also spoke of the island of Iona and Brude was pleased to donate it officially to Colmcille and his monks. Each day Colmcille told Colman that he had asked Brude to speak to Broichan about the release of Deirdre, without success.

Colman wandered around in a daze. He had come all this way to find his sister. Now he had found her but it did not seem possible to free her. Some day soon they would have to leave that place and he did not want to go. Thoughts whirled round in his head that he confided only to Diarmaid. Perhaps if he could find out where they were keeping Deirdre he could make some attempt to rescue her. Diarmaid always ended by telling him not to be so silly, that Colmcille would sort something out.

After they had been at King Brude's fort for a few weeks, Colmcille approached Colman one day,

'I'm afraid still no joy with Deirdre, Colman. But I have one more thing that I can try. Tomorrow we are set to leave, but not before a little surprise or two for Broichan, I think.' There was a twinkle in his eye which for once Colman did not find reassuring.

The feast on their last night surpassed even the first one that they had enjoyed after the baptism. The table groaned under the weight of plates of steaming broths and roast meat. And the smells were out of this world. For Colman there was no excitement at this feast as at the previous one. He glanced around the whole time, looking against all hope for his sister. But Broichan had kept her away this time.

Little passed between the Druid and Colmcille during the meal, each trying to commandeer the conversation with the King. After they had finished eating and pushed their plates away, Colmcille stood up and turning to the

156

King said 'Your majesty, I beg your permission to speak with your Druid and advisor, Broichan.'

The King smiled at him and nodded. He had enjoyed Colmcille's company over the last few weeks and would be sorry to see him go.

'Broichan,' said Colmcille, 'once more I entreat you, in the name of human decency, to release the slave girl, Deirdre, whom you took by force from her home and who is the only sister of one of my party.'

The Druid raised his head proudly. Colmcille had defeated him in most things since he had arrived at this fort. He had won the support of the King himself despite Broichan's own advice to the contrary. Here at last was one thing that Colmcille wanted and which was in Broichan's power to withhold. He smirked smugly and the sight of that grimace spreading slowly over the purple face was terrifying indeed to Colman. The boy shuddered and for a moment his whole world seemed to stop. The Druid was speaking now and his voice, confident in his hour of triumph, was even more terrible than the look on his face.

'It is surely no concern to the great Colmcille,' he sneered, almost spitting out the words, 'where I get my slaves or how. A slave is fairly taken by force or by barter. The girl you are interested in, however, is beyond barter price. You may if you wish, holy one, take her by force.' He laughed mockingly, knowing that Colmcille could or would do no such thing.

He made a signal to one of his guards and Deirdre was roughly brought back into the hall. Broichan stroked his moustache, delighting in having the upper hand.

'Now then,' he continued, ' did I say she was beyond price? Perhaps not, after all.' It was clear that a new thought had crossed his mind and he stroked his beard slowly and thoughtfully. 'If you and your party renounce your faith in the Christ and vow to follow the old ways again, I shall release her.'

Colman looked desperately at Colmcille. He didn't think that the abbot would ever do such a thing but looking at his face, it seemed as if he was indeed contemplating the proposition. For a moment time stood still for him. Of course he wanted Deirdre back at any price... almost, but not at the loss of Colmcille's integrity. Colmcille the abbot was what he believed in. For him to renounce his faith would be like losing his whole identity.

Colman jumped up, shouting 'No, Colmcille!' but the holy man merely looked at him blankly and raised an arm as if signalling him to keep quiet. Colman sat down slowly, his mouth drooping in dismay. Colmcille was speaking now.

'Broichan, this matter is in higher hands than ours,' he said and the quietness of his voice contrasted with the loudness of Broichan's previous outburst. 'Know this. If you have not handed over the slave girl freely and without hindrance by the time we have left King Brude's kingdom, you will suddenly die.' He bowed reverently towards Brude who had been listening to this exchange with interest. 'The noble king will bear witness to my words.'

He sat down. There was a hush over the hall as everyone looked to see what Broichan's reaction would be. He said nothing but with a kind of growl he stood up and strode out of the hall.

After they had gone there was an awkward silence. Brude clapped his hands for music and several minstrels came in, but it seemed to Colman and the monks from Iona that they sang only mournful tunes that night. On pretext of their long journey the next day, Colmcille asked if the King would let them go to bed early.

158

Colman didn't sleep but lay sobbing, wondering if there was any hope of Deirdre's return. It seemed that Colmcille had only been trying to force Broichan to hand over Deirdre with clever speaking. Now Broichan was going to call his bluff.

CHAPTER 12

Magic and Miracles

The next morning dawned brightly enough but for Colman it was a sorry parting. They said a cheerless goodbye to the King who was embarrassed at his inability to force Broichan to hand over Deirdre. They said their farewells too, to Haldo, who was going to stay on at his father's court. They had all grown fond of him during the journey and it was with heavy hearts that they said goodbye. For once, he seemed to have an inkling that there was something afoot, and there was not a smirk or a snigger to be seen on his face.

They were also laden with various treasures from King Brude as presents for the King of Dalriada. These were quite heavy but the first part of their journey was down hill, so that despite the extra weight they had to carry, they found it fairly easy and speedy going. Soon they had reached the river's edge.

Colman had not dared to speak to anyone, consciou

that their sympathy might overwhelm him and he would break down altogether. They began to walk along the path beside the river towards the loch. Suddenly Colmcille bent down as if he had caught sight of something on the ground. He took something out of the water and held it above his head. It was a white pebble. It glistened in the sunlight.

'Look at this white pebble, my friends. By it, God will cure many diseases among this heathen nation.' They looked from the pebble to each other. They were used to Colmcille's strange ideas by now but wondered what this could mean for them. They looked back at their leader. Colmcille was staring into the sky.

'The Druid Broichan is at this moment struck down with illness and near to death. An angel from heaven was sent to him which shattered the glass from which he was drinking, causing it to break into hundreds of pieces. He is at this moment gasping for breath, his throat and mouth torn to shreds.'

His followers looked at each other again. So Colmcille's prophecy had come true. Broichan was going to die because he hadn't given up the slave girl. It was Machar who spoke for them all.

'What will we do then, Colmcille?'

Colmcille glanced at him strangely as if unaware of the others.

'Well Machar, we shall wait here. At this very moment two messengers from the king are galloping down here to tell us that Broichan has consented to set the girl free.'

Colman had scarcely time to take all this in before two excited horsemen did indeed appear with that very message. They continued,

'King Brude now pleads with the holy Colmcille, if he has any compassion at all, to cure his advisor who, despite

161

his faults, has been a good friend to His Majesty. He is at death's door.'

Colmcille acted as if he had been expecting this request. He handed the pebble he had just found to Lugne.

'Take this, Lugne, to King Brude and tell him that if, first, Broichan promises to set the slave free, and then puts it in water and drinks from it, he shall be immediately cured. If he does not promise to free her he shall die right away.'

Colman stepped forward.

'Can I go too, Colmcille?' Colmcille looked at him.

'Please!' he pleaded.

'All right,' he nodded. 'It will help to have you there to bring Deirdre back. And Garbhan, you will have to go too to translate.'

With all speed the three ran back to Brude's fort. Colman hardly noticed the ground beneath his feet, so anxious was he to reach his sister. He ran well ahead of his two older companions. Even Lugne, strong athlete that he was, was forced to restrain him,

'Stop Colman, I have to get my breath!' But Colman would only let him pause for a short while. What if Broichan should die before they reached him? What then would happen to Deirdre? Would she be sacrificed in some awful druidic rite? He shuddered and put the thought firmly from him.

When they finally reached the fort they were ushered immediately by guards at the main gate into the big hall. Here Brude was restlessly pacing up and down while Broichan lay on a bed, blood running from his mouth. Beside him wiping his forehead with a cloth, was Deirdre. She looked up at the commotion caused by Lugne's entrance and her face lit up when she saw Colman too.

162

Lugne quickly related all that Colmcille had said and Garbhan translated breathlessly. Broichan could do nothing but moan but Brude immediately signalled for Deirdre to come forward, and he called for a smith to cut the fetters from her feet. Then he took the pebble that Lugne held out to him and threw it into a goblet of water.

Imagine everyone's surprise to see that the stone floated! Haldo, who had been hovering round them, clapped his hands with glee when he saw it. Brude tried to sink it but it refused to do anything but float. He took the goblet to Broichan and, raising the man's head, put the cup to his mouth.

At first it looked as though the Druid was going to be unable to drink but the stone floated down towards his lips and as soon as it touched them, first his eyes opened and then he began to drink noisily from the cup. As he drank, the blood around his mouth disappeared and by the time he had drunk only half of the water, he was sitting up as if nothing untoward had happened at all.

By this time Deirdre had returned with her fetters off, and Colman rushed towards her. As he held her in his arms he could hardly believe that it really was Deirdre. She said nothing to him but tears coursed down her face as she clung to him.

Suddenly there was a clatter. All eyes turned to see that Haldo had taken hold of the goblet and was drinking the remaining water.

'Haldo! What are you doing?' said Brude, even though it was too late to stop him.

Haldo was looking about him strangely now.

'Father!' he said slowly to King Brude. King Brude stared in astonishment.

'He remembers! Haldo! You remember!' He turned

slowly from his son and took the pebble out of the now empty goblet.

'It must be Colmcille's pebble. It has cured not only Broichan but Haldo as well!'

Brude held it out to Lugne in awe. 'You must take it back to him.'

Lugne shook his head.

'No! He said you could keep it. It can be used against any disease and sickness but it will not cure any illness if a man's appointed time for death has come.'

This was translated. Broichan exploded.

'You mean that my time of death hadn't really come! I have been conned!' and his face took on the colour of a thundery sky. He looked at Deirdre and was about to grab her back when Brude intervened.

'Broichan, a bargain is a bargain – certainly one struck under my roof. You will come with me and we will go and thank Colmcille for restoring your health and Haldo's senses and thank him too for the healing stone. Come, let the guards lead on!'

It was a stately procession that descended to the side of the river again. Despite the cure of his throat, Broichan grumbled the whole time that he had been tricked into giving up the slave girl and that of course it was what one would expect from someone like Colmcille. Colman following behind happily, hand in hand with Deirdre, paid no attention to him. He had his sister and all thoughts of revenge went out of his mind. What good would it do now? King Brude and Haldo walked arm in arm at the rear of the retinue, eagerly talking together and delighting in each other's company once more.

The monks were sitting around on the river bank when the Picts arrived. They greeted the royal procession and gathered round Colman to share his delight in the return of his sister.

Brude formally thanked Colmcille for the life of his druid and for the restoration of Haldo to his senses. Broichan merely grunted and muttered something.

'What's he saying?' said Diarmaid to Garbhan.

Garbhan shrugged his shoulders, 'He says that he'll show Colmcille yet that his druidic powers can be as great as Colmcille's own. He also asks what day will we set sail on Loch Ness?'

Colmcille replied that he had no powers of his own but that all things were ruled by God who was certainly more powerful than any Druid – even an Arch Druid, he added cheekily. He turned to Garbhan and asked,

'Garbhan, you know the route better than any of us. Which day shall we be sailing back down Loch Ness?'

'Tomorrow, hopefully,' replied Garbhan, ' – if we get going now!' he added pointedly.

When it was told him, Broichan stepped forward.

'Just to show you who has the stronger power,' he said quite unabashed, 'let me tell you that you will not sail tomorrow at all, for you will find that the winds are completely against you, and it will be so dark that it will be impossible to sail. Then you will know who holds the power! Come, we shall all accompany you to the head of the loch and we shall see what we shall see!'

'Broichan is certainly in a good humour now. There must have been something very powerful in that cure,' Diarmaid said to Colman as they started off on the journey to the loch. Colman paid no heed to Diarmaid, so engrossed was he in telling Deirdre all that had happened to him since they had been so roughly and suddenly parted. She listened carefully, her eyes clouding over as she learnt of the death of Cruithnechan but wide with wonder as she heard of all her brother's adventures since.

165

But when Colman asked how things had gone for her, she would say nothing.

The party camped for the night under a little shelter of heather and bracken used often by travellers taking this route. There was an air of merriment among Colmcille's monks and much singing that night. Broichan took himself off to one side and refused to join them but nobody cared. However, Colman was determined not to let Deirdre out of his sight as long as the old Druid was with them.

During the night the wind got up – a loud roaring that made Colman scared, and he nestled into his sister just as he had done in the old days. The whole night it seemed to increase so that even Comgall, who was lying close to Colman, began to get worried. Remembering the threat of the Druid to prevent their sailing, he glanced across at Colmcille who was sleeping soundly through the noise, a smile playing over his face. Surely this was the one night, if any, that Colmcille should have been up and out praying as he so often did when difficulties seemed about to beset them? The rest of the party lay awake, not speaking, listening to the awful sound of the storm outside. Would morning never come?

Suddenly Broichan appeared in the doorway. There was a crooked smile on his face. He said something in Pictish.

'He says it's morning,' said Garbhan, ' and why are we not up and ready for the journey that we plan to make?' The Druid was sniggering at his joke and said something more.

'Or perhaps we realise that Broichan's powers will be preventing us from going so we might as well stay in the shelter of this hut till his goodwill allows us the appropriate weather to sail.'

'Rubbish!' Colmcille had woken at the commotion and

jumped up. 'Make ready, my friends, for we leave very shortly.'

'But it's still dark!' said Diarmaid. 'It's pitch black out there!'

'It's morning and we are leaving right now!' commanded Colmcille.

Fearfully, his little band of followers pushed past the men of Brude's household who had accompanied them to this spot and went out into the darkness. It was so dark that they could not see the Druid's evil face once they were outside but they could hear him chuckling and could feel his evil presence.

'Launch the boats!' cried Colmcille above the wind which was blowing right down the loch at them. Halfheartedly the men pushed out their boats. This was madness indeed.

'Now raise the sails!' commanded their leader. They raised them but expected the masts to snap at any moment. Colmcille climbed into one of the boats. He stood in the stern.

'Push off!' he cried, and there was a note of triumph in his voice. Colman, Deirdre and Diarmaid sat in the same boat with him, huddled against the wind. How long would they have to wait till Colmcille managed to get the winds changed for them? It would probably take a lot of praying against Broichan's powerful magic and the darkness would not help.

Then suddenly Colman realised that they were moving in spite of the wind. They were moving straight into it! It was impossible! Even the darkness was lifting and he could look up and see that the sail was billowing into the wind. Impossible! He looked round. Beside them, the other boat was moving in a similar fashion and already the shore was well away from them. Suddenly, even as they sailed, the wind veered round and was now blowing them naturally down the loch without any loss of speed.

They could make out Broichan standing bemused and open-mouthed on the shingle. The crowd of foot soldiers standing watching and wondering on the beach beside him were just as amazed and began to laugh at Broichan, sneering just as much as they dared. But the wrath of the Druid was centred totally on the receding boats.

'You haven't hear the last of this, Colmcille!' shouted the Druid desperately. 'Mark my words! We shall meet again and you will know that druid magic can be stronger than yours. A curse on you and your party of travellers! You will be sorry indeed, before your journey is over, to have thwarted Broichan the Purple!

His threats were fading into the wind. Garbhan, who had been translating all this, turned to Colmcille and said,

'I can make out no more.'

Colmcille looked pleased. 'Probably just as well.'

'But what about his curse, Father?' asked Diarmaid worriedly.

The holy man smiled at him. 'Don't worry, we shall be protected. Nothing can be more powerful than the power of God in Christ.' He began slowly to sing a psalm, and as they recognised the words, the rest of the sailors joined in. Colman could imagine the fury of the Druid Broichan hearing them singing so lustily and already so far away, for they were speeding down the loch now. No need for the help of the Water Horse this time. They couldn't be going faster even if they tried!

Colman stopped singing and turned to Deirdre to tell her about the Water Horse but at that very moment there was a mighty whinny, and looking over the side of the boat, they could see the wild mane of their friend of the previous journey.

'Greetings, noble beast,' cried Colmcille. 'We meet again.'

'Greetings to you, holy Colmcille,' replied the Water Horse. 'I see that you have no need of my help today, but I will swim ahead of you just in case of any unforeseen dangers.

Colmcille laughed.

'Thank you, Water Horse, you are most thoughtful but I can assure you we have already come through the direst terrors today and the rest of our journey will be completely uneventful.'

He spoke the truth and they had easily reached the end of the loch by nightfall. The Water Horse took his leave of them and told them that if ever they were in trouble in his area any time in the future, to be sure and call upon him.

> 'The Mighty Water Horse
> can hear the faintest shout,
> can see the smallest speck
> and know what it's about!'

So saying, and with a final splash of his tail, he sank gracefully under the waves just as they made ready to land

Their friend Dorcan was out and waiting to greet them

'Well met again!' he cried with joy. 'I had my doubts tha' I would ever see any of you again. Come in, come in, anc tell us how you fared!'

He still seemed nervous and glanced uncertainl around just as he did the time before. Once they were i his little hut and telling him all that had happened sinc they had last seen him and how they had overcome th magic of Broichan and of Morrigan too, he seemed t relax a little.

At length he said,

'Well, am I glad to hear all your news, especially about Broichan. It is reassuring to hear that there is a power stronger than his evil magic. And what of Morrigan?' Even in the firelight's warm glow as he mentioned the name, a shiver of chill spread round the assembled company.

They all turned to Colmcille, themselves not sure of where Morrigan could be now. So taken up were they with Broichan, they had more or less forgotten all about her. They had not seen her since the day that Lugne had swum the river to fetch the boat over.

'Morrigan will be around, never fear ' said Colmcille. 'She will be with us until the end of the world, seeking whom she can with her grasping claws but she has no power against those who believe in the Christ.'

By the end of the evening Dorcan announced that he too believed in the Christ of Colmcille.

'Any God that is more powerful than Broichan and his magic must be powerful indeed. Mind, I'm not saying that if he appears again I shall be able to stand up to him, but who knows?'

'Who knows indeed?' said Colmcille smiling softly and the following morning before they left, he baptised Dorcan and his household in the very same well that he had blessed on the way to the Fortress of the Picts.

It was a lighthearted party that continued the homeward journey. Now away from Broichan's clutches, Colman was content to let Deirdre walk ahead with Garbhan who was telling her all about his life back at the Fortress of Dun Add. He also told her of his little daughter who would be waiting for him at home and of his wife who had been killed by marauders. Deirdre was sad for a while at hearing this. Although she had been captured too

171

by pirates, she realised how lucky she was not to have been killed too.

There was no sign of Morrigan that day and a feeling of happiness settled over the company. Even the weather stayed fair for them with exactly the right speed of wind for the loch journey.

They camped again at the spot where Colman and Colmcille had seen the bears. Colman stayed outside the whole night in the hopes of seeing them again, while Colmcille paced the shore in the moonlight, praying, but there was no sign of anything down by the lochside. The only sound to be heard above the lapping water was the howling of wolves in the forest, and even they did not seem so menacing now.

After his sleepless night, Colman slept soundly on the boat journey the next day. Even after they had come to the end of the loch and were well on their way back to Nesan's village, he walked as though in a dream. The whole thing had seemed a dream and he had to look round for Deirdre who was skipping along beside Garbhan to reassure himself that everything was in fact true.

He smiled happily. It was true! He and Deirdre were together once more and he would make sure that no-one ever took her away from him again. Colmcille had already told him that Iona could be his home forever. They would set up there in the safety of Colmcille's enclosure.

Colman was so wrapped up in his thoughts and plans that it was not until he stepped on the heels of Diarmaid who was walking in front of him, that he realised that the party had come to a halt. He peered over Diarmaid's shoulder.

Colmcille had stopped in his tracks and in front of him stood a ragged beggar who was dirty and unkempt. His face was bent down so that they could not really see it and

172

so it came as a surprise to hear Colmcille say,

'So, then we meet again! And I need hardly ask how things have gone with you. You didn't do as you were told, did you?' The beggar didn't look up and Colmcille beckoned to Garbhan to come from his place at the rear of the group and translate for him.

It was while Garbhan was speaking, that Colman suddenly realised that this was the beggar that Colmcille had presented with the magic stick on their journey to King Brude. He craned forward to catch the beggar's words as Garbhan translated for them all.

'He says that at first he did just as the holy Colmcille had told him, and had placed the stick in the forest. Every night some wild beast or other had fallen upon it and died so that they had plenty to eat and to spare for their neighbours. But his wife wasn't happy and persuaded him that he ought to hide the stick in case a child or someone's cow should become impaled on it. Then they would be liable to pay the punishment which would be imprisonment for the whole family at the very least, or perhaps even death for them all.'

The beggar paused, seeming unsure as to how he would continue. Colmcille said nothing but kept a steely eye on him. At length the beggar, seeing that he was getting no sympathy from that quarter, continued, stammering. Garbhan explained.

'He told his wife that the stake would do no such thing as it had been blessed by the holy Colmcille. But she would hear nothing of it so at length he gave in to her and took the stake out of its position in the forest and stood it against the wall in the house. Imagine their horror the next day when they discovered that their dog had fallen upon it. His wife went berserk and shrieked at him to get it out of the house before one of the children was killed by it. So he took it to the thickest part of the forest where he hid it under some brushwood. The next day he went back just to check and found to his dismay that a young doe had managed to fall upon it and was dead. He then hid it at the edge of a river and the following day a salmon was impaled on it. He was scarcely able to carry the fish home, it was so big, but was his wife pleased? She was not. She made him put the stake up on the roof of their house where the children couldn't get near it. Almost as soon as he had done so a crow alighted on it and fell dead instantly. The woman became so worried about it that she plagued her husband to chop it up and burn it. This he did and now he has nothing again and begs for alms.'

The beggar was shaking his head. 'He doesn't want anything magical this time, he says. Just a few straightforward alms.'

Colmcille stood for a while still staring at the dejected man.

'I might have known this would happen, ' he said eventually. He addressed the man. 'Go,' he said. 'I gave you a priceless gift and you had not the faith to sustain it. How would you cope with anything less? I tell you now to go to your wife and ask her to remedy your situation, since you seem to value her instructions above mine.'

And he raised his head and walked straight past the man before Garbhan had even finished translating.

Colman turned to Diarmaid. 'That was a bit hard on the man, wasn't it?'

Diarmaid shrugged.

'Colmcille doesn't suffer fools gladly.' So saying, he too hurried off after his master and Colman followed slowly, watching with the rest of the party as the beggar retreated dejectedly into the forest once again.

They carried on walking. As they went, something

began to worry Colman. He was not sure at first what it was. Something was niggling at the back of his mind. He was still wondering what it could be when there was a shrieking on the path ahead of them. He stiffened with fear. It was getting dark. Was it a banshee?

CHAPTER 13

The Final Parting

The shrieking came towards them alarmingly quickly. Colman looked round automatically for Deirdre – she who had always been his shelter from danger throughout his life. She was not far behind him in the column but was deep in conversation with Garbhan and had not noticed the wailing.

As the noise grew louder, Colman suddenly realised that it was coming from a human rather than a supernatural being and as the person came into view, he saw that it was none other than their good friend Nesan the Crooked.

Nesan ran up to them and threw himself on his knees in front of Colmcille. Colmcille bent and helped the old man to his feet. There were tears streaming from Nesan's face and, alarmed, they wondered what on earth could be causing him so much grief. As he stammered his greetings at them, they suddenly realised that the weird noises they had heard had been shrieks of joy.

After a while, when they had managed to calm the man down, they heard that each of his heifers had, in the few weeks since they passed that way and Colmcille had blessed them, given birth to twenty calves. Already Colmcille's prophecy had been fulfilled!

Colmcille smiled delightedly and Nesan skipped ahead of them in spite of his crippled leg and bad back till they reached his village where everyone was out to greet the party.

Nothing would do but Nesan must first show them the calves. He had them in an enclosure beside his house. Colmcille fondled them carefully, laughing at Nesan and his excitement.

'Why are you so overcome, Nesan?' he smiled, 'surely you believed that my prediction would happen?'

'Well, yes,' said Nesan, 'I thought your predictions would come true. But didn't think that it would happen so fast. Why, these cows weren't even in calf when you were here! It's just impossible for a cow to produce one healthy calf in such a short time, never mind twenty!'

Colmcille laughed again.

'Nesan, we shall make a Christian of you yet! It is written in our holy writings that with God all things are possible. It seems so clear and so obvious but even people who see wonders such as this will fail to believe.' He put an arm round the man's shoulder. 'Come, we are tired and hungry. May we use your hospitality yet again?'

Nesan could not do enough for them that evening. After a good meal, they sat long into the night hours telling Nesan and his family all that had happened to them and all about the court of the High King of the Picts. Colman listened to it all and was careful this time to give the heather ale a miss when it was offered to him.

The next day Nesan gave them a cheery farewell as they loaded themselves into the boats. It was a relief to Colman to know that the days of carrying the boats over long distances was now over. They would travel back today to the Isle of Lìos Mòr, then on to their beloved Iona. Everything was perfect. Nothing could go wrong now.

However, as they sailed that day over choppy waters, Colman realised at last what had been worrying him at the back of his mind. He had already decided that he and Deirdre would set up home in Iona and he had hoped that life would be happy and carefree again but it came to him now that there were not any women in the enclosure at Iona. Could a place be found there for Deirdre? She was his sister and he loved her and needed her.

He made up his mind that he would broach the subject with Colmcille that very night.

As was his custom, Moluag greeted them with flamboyant hospitality and insisted on washing their feet on arrival as he had done on their previous visit.

'Never a one to be outdone, eh Moluag?' teased Colmcille. Nevertheless they had walked a long way since they had last seen Moluag and their feet welcomed the attention. In his turn, Moluag was interested to learn of their journey and especially of Haldo's cure.

'I always thought that perhaps something could be done for him ' he mused, 'But I knew it wouldn't be here.' His eyes twinkled merrily above his silver beard as he added, 'Life is always so full of surprises!'

Again they talked far into the night and it was pleasant, after all these weeks, to be able to understand the whole conversation without Garbhan or anyone else having to translate. Poor Garbhan fell asleep early on in the evening. Exhaustion finally overtook him now that they no longer depended on him for translating or showing the way.

Deirdre cradled his head as he slept and at the sight of it, Colman was reminded that he had to speak to Colmcille about her.

When everyone decided it was time to settle down for the night, he approached Colmcille.

'Father, may I talk with you a moment?'

Colmcille gave him one of his piercing looks.

'Yes, Little Colm,' he said. 'Come with me and we shall take a walk. It's a lovely evening for it.'

It was indeed a beautiful evening, warm and balmy, with the rustle of water lapping against the shore. The moon glinted across the sea making a pattern like delicate trellis work.

Colman wondered how he was going to say it.

'It's about Deirdre,' he blurted out.

'Yes,' said Colmcille, not sounding particularly surprised.

'It's about... well... I was wondering. Well you see, you remember when I first came to Iona and you said that I could make it my home now, seeing that Broichan and his evil band had destroyed my only other home...'

'Yes,' encouraged Colmcille.

'Well, I have decided that I do want to stay in Iona with you and I want to become one of your monks. Would be all right if Deirdre came to stay there too?' He paused to draw breath. 'You see, if I go to Iona she is going to be all on her own and I don't think she realises this yet.'

'You mean you haven't spoken to her about this?' said Colmcille softly.

'Well, no. I wanted to clear it with you first. I haven't even told her that I want to be a monk. You see, I think he wants me to be a warrior like my father and avenge those who killed him.'

Colmcille paused a moment, then said,

179

'I think you should speak to your sister about all this. You see, Little Colm, it is one of our monastic rules that no women be allowed in the enclosure.' He shrugged. 'It can't be broken for you or anyone.'

Colman was crestfallen. He had not expected this.

'But Colmcille, she could be a help. She used to look after me and Cruithnechan. She could look after your monks. Then they'd have plenty of time for prayer and...'

'No!' cut in Colmcille angrily. He had never been angry with Colman before and the boy was taken aback. As soon as he'd said it, Colman sensed that the abbot regretted it for his voice softened. 'It is just one of our rules, Little Colm. One day you'll understand. Besides, we have plenty of willing and capable men to look after the monks of Iona. I want you to go in now and talk to your sister and see what she says. After all, it is her future. She must be consulted. Now go, I have to pray.'

Colman was so surprised at Colmcille's vehemence that he went without a further word but tears were stinging his eyes. Just when he had thought they were safe and secure again there was going to be no haven for them on Iona.

When he got back to Moluag's hospice, Deirdre was still just awake, leaning sleepily against the wall with Garbhan's head still cradled in her lap.

Colman whispered to her so as not to waken the others who were lying around.

'Can you come a minute, Deirdre? I must speak to you.'

She looked up and seeing the tears that seemed about to erupt in his eyes, she quickly and gently pushed Garbhan's head away and extricated herself enough to squeeze out from the sleeping bodies to where Colman waited for her. He beckoned her to go outside with him.

They walked hand in hand in the opposite direction from that taken earlier by Colman and Colmcille. Colman took no delight now in the warmth of the evening or the sound of the water on the shore.

Quickly he told her how he wanted to be a monk and follow Colmcille and to live with her forever on Iona. She stopped dead and in the darkness, he felt, rather than saw, her face fall. Well, he knew it would come as a shock to her to learn that he wanted to become a monk.

'Oh Colman,' she said sadly 'that can't be. I can't live on Iona with you.' She ruffled his hair as she used to do in the old days. So, she knew about Colmcille's rules then! She must have been expecting that they would go back to Ireland after all. He could feel her hesitating.

'Colman,' she continued. 'This is not easy for me to say for I know how much you depend on me but... well... Garbhan has asked me to go with him to Dun Add and be his wife, and look after his little girl.'

It was Colman's turn to be shocked. With Garbhan? But Deirdre was his sister! She held his shoulders firmly.

'Colman, you are a big boy now and able to make your own way in the world. You don't really need me any more. I am delighted that you want to join Colmcille in Iona. You will have a home and a family with the monks and we won't be so very far away from each other. But Garbhan needs me now and I have already promised to go with him.'

It seemed that that was all there was to say. Colman was so stunned by the turn of events that he did not know whether to be happy or sad. Now he could live in Iona as he had planned and Deirdre had a home where she would be happy. And after all as she said, it was not so very far away.

Deirdre went back into the hut and Colman went straight off in the other direction to tell Colmcille. He found the abbot down by the shore and told him the outcome of this talk with Deirdre. He also said what a shock it had been to him to find that Deirdre had been making her own plans.

'I guessed as much, Colman,' was all the abbot would comment. 'Life often has its own way of working out for the best!'

The following morning various plans were mooted as to what they would do next. Colmcille said that he was worried about Iona for they had been away from it for a very long time. He was anxious to go there first to check that everything was still in order. After a few days, if everything was as he hoped, he would pay a visit to King Conall and tell him how things had gone at the court of the Picts.

Garbhan wanted to go straight home to Dun Add. They didn't need him any more and he wanted to see his daughter again. He didn't want to waste time going to Iona first... and then of course there was Deirdre.

Cainnech and Comgall had had enough, they said. They were getting old and didn't want to go anywhere for the time being! The discussion got quite heated, and at length it was Moluag who stepped in with the solution.

'Cainnech and Comgall, why don't you stay with me a while,' he suggested. 'You're more than welcome as company. Then Garbhan can take Deirdre home to Dun Add in one of your boats and the rest of you can travel in the other boat to Iona.'

The solution seemed simple once it had been said.

They got the boats ready and Colman realised suddenly that this was the real moment of goodbye for himself and Deirdre. He had given everything he had over the last few weeks to rescue his sister, thinking that life would go back to normal once she returned. Now it seemed that life would never be the same for him again. He fought back